ALAN SAWNER

ALAN SAWNER

RISING SHADOWS

WILLIAM SILVER

PARTRIDGE
A Penguin Random House Company

Print information available on the last page.

To order additional copies of this book, contact
Partridge India
000 800 10062 62
orders.india@partridgepublishing.com

www.partridgepublishing.com/india

CONTENTS

Chapter 1

CONFIDENCE IS THE KEY

Grim…it was the first word that came to Scottish businessman, Alan Sawner's mind as he stepped out of the Soekarna-Hatta international airport in Jakarta. The clouds looming above were the same shade of grey as Alan's designer suit. The purple tie was a good touch. His dark brown eyes zeroed in on a black limousine that was driving into the terminal. The expensive car pulled up in front of him and the Asian chauffeur rushed to open the door. Once he was in, the man loaded his employer's luggage into the trunk. The car began moving slowly down the asphalt road and soon started driving towards the city.

Once it left the airport premises, the car was instantly swept away by the bustling, 3'o clock traffic. Alan tapped his Acer laptop nervously. He absolutely could not afford to be late for this meeting. Too much was at stake here. This was truly the most expensive joint venture he had ever attempted. Several thoughts ran through the billionaire's mind…the expedition itself was extremely risky, his surprise would definitely convince the investors, but was his life worth the reward if he succeeded? That was a big *if*. Then again he had always loved challenges.

The analytical part of his mind rehearsed his plan for the presentation. He had always possessed the ability to imagine an event before it actually happened, like a presentation, and guess the possible outcomes, preparing for each. He was now busy checking that his calculations were right and the funds would be enough, down to a single digit.

Meanwhile the creative part wondered as to what was there in the Chorés that made it a place of fear and what secrets awaited to be discovered. This island held the answers to so many questions. He would be the one to discover them.

Alan remembered a story, an incident rather, to be more accurate. It had made big news in the Hong Kong newspapers. A boy, Christopher Marques along with his brother Erik and his parents were visiting one of the six outer islands of the Tenebris Chorés. The outer islands were considered completely safe and were famous tourist attractions, as that was the closest one could get to the actual island where things started going wrong. The boy's elder brother had a demented idea to take the boat that they had arrived in for a visit to the main island. Through dumb luck, they managed to steal the boat after the captain and other passengers (including their parents) had disembarked. The elder of the two, Erik steered the boat while his brother, Christopher or Chris for short, filmed the journey.

Chris had later sent a letter to Alan to warn him of the dangers there once word of his expedition got out.

Initially the boys had been safe, but when Chris reached the edge of the forest, he had blacked out. He described feeling unbearable pain and had supposedly had visions of massive fires and floods ravaging cities.

Erik on the other hand had abandoned his brother when he saw Chris rise magically into the air and dissolve into white mist. Though Chris swore that none of his brother's accounts of the event matched his own, Erik was equally firm in what he believed he had seen.

Chris had left his camera back on the island which had still been filming. If only that could have been retrieved, a huge breakthrough would have been made in discovering the secrets of the island.

Chris had been found four months later, drifting in the sea, by a search party. According to Christopher, he had been gone only a few hours.

The first time that Alan had read this letter...he had experienced a mixture of feelings, such as curiosity, disbelief, excitement, uncertainty and suspicion to name a few.

The more he read it, the more it made sense to him. His expert analysts presented several theories to explain the events and quite a few appealed to him.

"Hurry up, will you Jimmy?" said Alan in a British accent.

"I absolutely cannot be late for this meeting."

"Don't worry, sir, I have never been late."

"I trust you, but this is of too much importance."

"Just relax, sir, we'll be at the hotel soon."

Alan finally decided that he was as ready as he would ever be. He calmed himself down and muttered to himself, "Confidence is the key."

His eyes wandered and set themselves on the traffic jam outside. Progress was painstakingly slow. Finally a ray of hope shown from a gap in the clouds just as the traffic cleared and the car picked up speed.

Alan looked at the bustling city outside. There was utter confusion. Lental Jenderal street was filled with supermarkets, apartments, houses, skyscrapers and hotels. Different aspects of a metropolis put together in one street. He looked at school buses bringing children home, taxis bringing tourists to their hotels, families walking to the supermarkets and a lone man on a bicycle pedaling through the heavy, but fast moving traffic.

At last Alan Sawner's destination came into view. It was a fourteen storey white building and a board on top, displaying a white letter 'R' on a dark background with five white stars above it. Below it, again in white text where the words 'The Royal Group of Hotels: Jakarta.' The extravagant five star hotel belonged to Mr Alan Sawner.

Alan checked the time on his custom-made, handcrafted, platinum Rolex. It was 4'o clock. He had arrived with five minutes to spare. "Great driving Jimmy..." he told his loyal driver, "and about that salary raise of yours, you can have it." "Tha...thank you sir." the driver stammered, but Alan has already gotten off with his laptop and was bolting towards the main entrance.

The ground floor had white granite tiles and beige walls which were decorated with great taste. The side walls were lined with the entrances of several multi- cuisine restaurants. The head wall was curved and a black granite reception desk ran the entire width of the hall. There was a white marble fountain in the centre. It had two escalators with the fountain between them. There were four elevators, two on either side of the reception desk.

The hotel was organized extremely well. Alan himself designed the interior of each of his ninety-two hotels across forty-eight countries. The first floor had a corridor which jutted out from the side walls and above the reception area. It had the doors to the twenty rooms which were located on that floor. The other twelve floors had the same design. Except the fourteenth one, which had ten luxury class suites and a conference room, which was where Alan was going.

"Good evening sir." said Colin Miller, an Australian with bright blue eyes and sandy hair. He pretty much had the looks of a cool, carefree surfer. Few would believe that he was a billionaire's secretary. He caught up to Alan at the elevator door and stepped in after greeting him. "Are the guests here yet?" enquired Alan. "Mr Varma, Mr Brenorski, Sheik Halmeer and Mr Phillepe have arrived. Mr Lai Chee Yen has just entered Lental Jenderal street."

"Good, have you arranged the projector and sound systems I asked for Colin?" asked Alan. "Yes sir, Mr Sawner." replied Colin. "You don't always have to be so formal Colin. I just behave that way for the sake of my business." Though he liked to think otherwise, Alan had always been well mannered and overly formal by nature.

The Toshiba elevator came to a halt. The two men stepped out and walked towards the conference room through automatic glass sliding doors which had motion sensors attached to a scanner above it. The room was heavily air conditioned. It had white walls on three sides and a huge window on one, which overlooked the crowded metropolis below. The entire floor was covered with a black carpet. In the centre of the room was a resin-coated, carbon fiber conference table. It was elliptical and white in colour with six glasses of fresh spring water placed on it. There were six chairs of the same material as the table, only with black leather cushions on them. Four of them were occupied. There was also a projector suspended from the roof. No screen would be required as the walls themselves were the purest of white.

"Good evening gentlemen, it is my honour to have you here, we may begin our meeting as soon as Mr Lai Chee Yen arrives." Alan stated and as though on cue the doors slid open and a short stubby man entered. His grey hair and dark eyes, reminded Alan of one of his professors from Oxford.

He walked briskly for his age and sat down. Alan then shook each individual's hand firmly. One must never underestimate the value of a well executed handshake.

First in line was Mr Rahul Varma, a thirty-eight year old Indian who had established his billion dollar empire in the fields of software and robotics. He had brown hair and coffee coloured eyes which matched his tie. Alan shook Victor Brenorski's hand next. Victor was a successful man in the shipping industry. Alan then shook Sheik Halmeer al-Jilani's hand. He was an oil tycoon from the U.A.E dressed in a dark blue suit. Then it was Montres Phillepe's turn. He owned an airline called 'Gold Wing Air'. Last in line was Mr Lai Chee Yen, who was the owner of the Lifecare chain of hospitals.

Alan walked over to the empty chair and stood beside it. He placed his laptop on the table and typed in the password. He clicked a few times and sat down. "Gentlemen...please enjoy the show." Alan looked at Colin who was standing near the entrance

5

and nodded. Colin spoke into a small microphone and the projector flickered into life.

An image of Alan was projected onto the wall, his voice spoke through the hidden speakers in the roof, "Gentlemen, I am sure all of you know why you are here, then again as the host it is my duty to repeat what I said over the phone.

I Allan Sawner, have planned to send an expedition to unravel the secrets of the Tenebris Chorés or in English, the Dark Lands. But to do so I need your assistance. As in every joint venture, the profits will be shared. All I request is a mere ten million dollars from each of you. I am convinced that it is a small amount to pay compared to the knowledge that will be uncovered. If your opinions differ, I am firm in the belief that the expedition team and plan that I have put together will change your views."

"Before I reveal the expedition crew I would like to elaborate the reason behind my confidence." A picture of the islands appeared next to Alan's image on the wall. The six smaller islands surrounding the larger central island appeared green, they were safe to travel to and were popular tourist destinations. The main island itself was displayed in red. A blue line cut through its heart. "The blue line represents the safe path charted by my analysts, several expert astrophysicists, geologists and technical engineers making use of the entrances in the cliff wall, something never tried before, to chart a course right through the centre..." explained Alan's projection.

"But the team I have chosen is the true reason for my belief that this expedition will succeed." Alan's voice was still audible but his image and the projection of the islands disappeared to be replaced by the picture of a man in his early twenties with curly dark hair, wearing sunglasses that covered his brown eyes. He was dressed in a black suit and was wearing a grey trench coat standing in some sort of class room. Some written information was shown next to the image.

"As I am sure all of you are aware, this is the image of Dr Delton Kraig, the first member of the expedition crew." The investors started nodding and few gently clapped. Alan's voice began again, "Dr Kraig is probably the most well renowned astrophysicist of our time. He graduated at the Berkley university (with honours) at the young age of twenty-two with a PhD. He was imme-diately recruited by N.A.S.A and set an unofficial record by being promoted seven times in the span of one year.

At the age of twenty-three, a year ago, he headed the Bermuda triangle expedition and unraveled one of the greatest mysteries on planet Earth. Now to solve another such mystery there is no one more apt than Dr Kraig. Now we know that there is a gravitational anomaly in the triangle that caused the disappearances. We believe there is something similar in the Tenebris Chorés islands."

Alan was enjoying himself, he had the undivided attention of the room's occupants. His voice started off once again. "The second member of the expedition crew is none other than Mr Patrick Maple." Again, nods and claps from the investors, though one of them seemed a bit disturbed. "All of us know this man…" Delton's image was replaced by a man with blonde hair and bright blue eyes wearing faded jeans, a white polo neck shirt and a dark blue casual blazer. The white Adidas loafers created a striking contrast. He was photographed while walking in Times Square, New York.

"This individual won the Nobel prize for his Mars colonization project. His idea to send a calculated, weak nuclear bomb to the core of the red planet to increase its rotation and recreate its magnetic field was a stroke of pure genius. Now, even as I speak, Machines are releasing greenhouse gases to increase Mars's surface temperature. His expertise in geology will make a valuable addition to the expedition crew."

Alan felt more relaxed. *Now that they are mostly convinced, do I have to do it?*, he thought to himself. The image changed again. Alex Maple was wearing denim jeans with a red short sleeve shirt which had 'rock n roll' on it in white letters. He was sitting on the steps of some ancient stone building.

"Gentlemen, you are now looking at the greatest inventor of the century, Mr Alex Maple. He is the brother of Mr Patrick Maple who is part of the crew as well. All expeditions require cutting edge technology and who better to design them than twenty-four year old Mr Maple. His innovations have brought about a new age of human technology. It is my strong belief that he is a vital part of this crew."

The glass doors slid open and a waiter came in with six cups of earl grey tea and cookies. He placed it on the table and rushed out. Alan frowned, none of them had even noticed the cookies, so rude. Perhaps his presentation was that good.

The image changed one more time. Now it showed a slim woman, with auburn hair and hazel eyes, standing in what was apparently a greenhouse. She was wearing a white lab coat and protective goggles.

Alan had recorded the video over a month ago and knew what was next, "This gentlemen…is Dr Martha Frost. It is my firm belief that getting readings of the anomalies on the island is just as important as understanding how plants and animals are affected by them. For this purpose, Dr Frost shall be a valuable member of the crew."

The image changed for the final time, now it showed a man in a yellow trucking outfit, scaling the side of a cliff. His dark hair was covered by a helmet, his light brown eyes glistened and he wore a broad grin on his face.

"Gentlemen, this is the fifth member of the crew, world famous actor, adventurer, businessman and my close friend, Mr Andrew Briston. Mr Briston and I graduated from the Oxford university in London in the same year. He is my close friend and will definitely be an essential crew member. His various other expeditions in several places around the world has equipped him with knowledge and expertise that will be needed for this one. I am confident that I have convinced you to invest in this venture." ended Alan's recorded voice.

It took Alan's investors a second to realize that the presentation has ended, they began clapping loudly and appreciating Allan. They were convinced enough, did he have to commit? *Better safe than sorry*, Alan thought to himself, "Gentlemen, there is a sixth member, his name is Alan Sawner." There was an instant wave of questions.

"Gentlemen, please calm down. I value my life greatly and would not risk it if I wasn't absolutely certain. This should give you enough reason to invest in me." The first of them began. "Mr Brenorski and I had our doubts but now we are prepared to invest." said Mr Varma. Two down, three to go. Mr Lai Chee Yen spoke next, "I have decided that it is in the best interests of Mr Phillepe and myself to invest in this venture." Great, now Alan had the necessary funds for the expedition. Mr Jilani's investment was just an extra backup fund to afford for any setbacks.

"I am not prepared to invest," said Sheik Halmeer al-Jilani. "there is a reason why no one has ever returned from there. Some things are better left alone. Humans are not ready to discover its secrets yet. You may unleash something in there that could put an end to several lives, I do not want that on my conscience."

Alan wasn't too worried, he had prepared for this, "Sheik Halmeer, if humans had thought that electricity was better left alone, we wouldn't have advanced medical equipment. Would you say that is better? Many said the same about the Bermuda triangle, but the expedition was successful. Please don't be so superstitious." "Maybe you are right Mr Sawner, but I do not wish to invest." Alan decided that he would have to manage without the emergency fund, "I understand…for those who are investing, if I do not return, your investment will be returned to you by my company."

Everyone including the Sheik clapped and they left the conference room together, followed by Colin, who still wondered why Mr Sawner hadn't used a HD screen instead of a projector. Well sometimes he was known to be nostalgic.

They decided to finish lunch at one of the multi-cuisine restaurants. As they ate, the main topic of conversation was the island. The Sheik preferred to keep quite as the others spoke.

Alan had to maintain his role as a person with a lot of knowledge about the island. Often even exaggerating details. After all, he was talking with his investors. If he had learnt one thing over the years, it was that you had to be in character even if the presentation was over, leaving no chance for doubt.

They took the elevator down and walked towards the exit of the hotel. Six cars came down the driveway to pick up a billionaire each. Sheik Halmeer left, after bidding them farewell, in a white Rolls Royce. Then a valet stepped out of a Lamborghini, handed Mr Phillepe the keys, and left. The billionaire raced away. Then a white BMW picked Victor Brenorski and was off. Finally Rahul Varma left in a silver Mercedes Benz. Mr Chee Yen shook Alan's hand one last time and was gone in a black Land Rover. Finally Jimmy arrived in Alan's limousine.

In a few minutes, the man with big dreams was heading back to the Soekarna-Hatta international airport. After leaving Lental Jenderal street, Jimmy turned a sharp right and asked, "How was the meeting sir?" "Fantastic," answered Alan.

Meanwhile, at the National Tsunami Warning Centre or NTWC for short, a newly appointed officer failed to notice an underwater earthquake which registered a whopping 7.8 on the Richter scale.

This mistake would cost the lives of millions, but it was necessary (This sentence may sound weird, but everything will be explained). There was nothing any human could have done about it. The creators had planned it this way.

Alan stared out of his window. A white car was driving by. He looked into the car and saw a familiar face, a face he had expected to see only in Germany a few days later. It came as quite a surprise but it was a mere speck compared to the surprise that nature held in store for him. He yelled, "Stop the car!"

Chapter 2

REVELATION

The face that Alan Sawner had seen belonged to his friend from college and fellow expedition crew member, Andrew Briston. Alan's chauffeur driven limousine turned right and came to a halt on the highway, blocking the path of Andrew's BMW.

Andrew looked the same as he had in his trucking photograph, except for the fact that he was dressed in a black suit, with a white shirt and a sky blue tie. The two men looked at each other for a second, then shook each other hands warmly and embraced. There was a gentle breeze playing across the grass on either side of the highway. Then it stopped abruptly just as the men let go and started laughing. There was no breeze for a long time, like the calm before a storm, but what was coming was much worse than a storm.

"How are you Alan? It seems like an eternity ago that I last saw you face to face." Andrew said. "Never better...just in case you forgot, you saw me just eleven months ago in January." Andrew laughed and began talking again, "I do remember Alan, but we used to see each other everyday at college. Comparatively, that's quite a difference." Alan replied with a slightly thoughtful expression, "You do have a point there Andrew."

"How come you're in Jakarta now? I was supposed to pick you up in Germany." said Alan. "Well…I just received news that Martha moved to France, so I came to tell you." Alan raised his left eyebrow and smiled slyly, "You could have just called or sent an e-mail." "I doubt you could have found my e-mail in the tens of thousands that you get every day…" Alan still kept his expression and Andrew sighed, "fine, I wanted to come along when you gave our fellow crew members the good news." Alan nodded, it was typical of Andrew. Be it the result of a competition or the names of selected members for their 'Literature club' in college, Andrew loved to be present when the results were announced. It gave him a sort of awkward satisfaction.

"When is your flight scheduled?" asked Andrew. "Three hours from now, I was just heading to the airport when I saw you and told Jimmy to stop."

"Jimmy?"
"My driver."
"I have a mansion by the coast, we can go there."
"Is it too far?"
"No."
"Alright, we can go in my car."
"My house, my ride."

The two businessmen climbed into the white BMW. Alan lowered the power window and said to his driver, "Jimmy, take the car back to the airport and then you can have the rest of the day off." "Thank you Mr Sawner." said the driver, barely containing his pleasure at having the day off, maybe he could take his family out for dinner now that he had a pay raise too. This was proving to be a very surprising day. What Jimmy didn't realize was that the day wasn't over yet and more surprises laid in store.

"Let's go Henry." said Andrew to his driver. "Where to sir?" asked the driver with a strong Australian accent. "The mansion please Henry." Andrew had a British accent too but it was much deeper than Alan's, who still had a slight Scottish influence in his speech. "Well, how have you been?" "Good," replied Andrew, "phenomenal actually, my stocks are rising but most importantly there's a new adventure awaiting. Brief me on our plan again."

"Alright then," began Alan "firstly we must exclude Dubai from our flight plan as Martha is no longer there.

In three hours we'll be taking my private jet to Portland in the U.S. We shall be meeting Dr Kraig in one of his universities there. After his 2'o clock lecture, we shall be finishing lunch at my hotel and will stay there till 5'o clock. From there we shall be going to New York city where we'll meet Patrick at his lab the next day. Again we'll be taking a few hours off to rest.

We shall then be flying to Paris where we'll collect Alex and Martha. According to Alex he still needs four days to prepare his equipment. Which means we will have to stay in Paris for a day. I think it'll also be a good time for everyone to prepare themselves mentally for the journey ahead.

We would have visited Dubai but as you said, Martha isn't there so we shall be directly heading to Hong Kong, stopping in Dubai only to refuel. We'll arrive in the evening, so we can get a good night's sleep before the journey begins. In the morning, a press meet will be held to mark the historic day.

Finally we will have to take a boat ride to the fourth island which is the closet to the central one as I previously told you over the phone. Then a boat carrying our specially modified transportation will take us to the main island's South face where the opening in the cliff wall gives us easy access to the forest. Then what happens next is a mystery."

"Perfect," Andrew said, "though the mystery part does make me a little nervous." "Everyone is pretty nervous. It's not just a walk in the park, but just imagine the answers we'll find, the undivided attention of the world will be focused on us. If we succeed, it will be a glorious day indeed." "Let's hope you're right Alan, you do realize that if you're wrong, it might cost us our lives." "It's difficult enough to carry that burden without you reminding me." Alan replied in a low tone.

They travelled in silence after that. It had been half an hour since they had met on the highway when they arrived at the beach. It was plain except for a tall steeply rising cliff to the right and a white mansion at the bottom of it. It was apparently the only mansion there and could only have been Andrew's. It was two storied and 'L' shaped. The main entrance was rather magnificent. Two large heavy wooden doors guarded the many treasures inside, which would soon mean nothing. There were several windows neatly arranged in grids. The other part which formed a ninety degree angle, had curved arches. There were no walls between the arches and the they formed a sort of veranda. The second floor of that part of the mansion was normal.

Alan whistled and said, "Impressive." "Welcome to my humble residence." said Andrew with a formal bow. "The view from the lighthouse is very good." commented Andrew staring at the top of the cliff. Alan didn't understand how he hadn't noticed the massive stone column. It seemed very old and it was indeed.

Just then the ground shook violently and the men were thrown off their feet. Then the trembling stopped all of a sudden. "Earthquakes are quite common in Jakarta right?" asked Alan, pretty concerned. "Yeah pretty much, but…" Andrew's words faded away. They watches with growing terror as the ocean water retreated, exposing coral reefs and leaving fish jumping about in the sand. A tsunami was seconds away. They had a minute at the most.

"The mansion." yelled Andrew and began sprinting. There was no time for questions but if there was, Alan would have asked what good a mansion might do against a tsunami, but he just ran. They still had about a hundred yards to go when another earthquake struck.

The lighthouse could not withstand this one. It crumpled and toppled over the cliff. As it is with every hero's luck, it landed on the mansion, crushing it like a tin can. The cliff had been so high that the lighthouse had gained enough momentum to level the mansion. Andrew swore and crashed down to the ground. Alan came to a stumbling halt beside his friend. "What…happened?"

he gasped. "There was a tsunami bunker in the mansion, a tunnel leads far inland. We would have been safe." Andrew swore again.

To their horror a wall of water rose above their heads. Their feet turned to lead. Andrew wanted to say something. A goodbye... anything, but he couldn't muster the courage to say it. Not even the faintest hint of hope shown on their faces as the wave came crashing down and everything went dark, but they were nowhere close to the end, far from it as a matter of fact.

When he regained consciousness, Alan had an awkward feeling, not pain...this was different, he couldn't find a word for it. Where was he, how did he get there and most importantly *who* was he? Then his memories came rushing back like a second tsunami. He remembered his meeting in Jakarta, his expedition, meeting Andrew on the way then the tsunami. After his memories set themselves right to some extent and he could think clearly again, his first thought was, *Am I dead?*

The answer to that question was that he was and he wasn't. He had been inexplicably transported to a dimension where time was irrelevant. He was in the same timeline as his birth, life and death. Though he knew none of this, so he might as well be two years old and dead at the same time.

Finally as the last of his memories set in, he found the word to define what he felt. It was weightlessness. His eyes were closed and it felt like an eternity to open them. In that dimension, he actually might have. He slowly raised his eyelids, afraid of what he might see.

Alan Sawner was floating in mid-air. He couldn't tell which way was up or down because there was absolutely no gravity. It was as if he was in space, except in space he would not be able to breathe unless he had an oxygen tank strapped to his back or if he was in a space shuttle. Neither of which was apparently visible. He took in his surroundings. There wasn't much. It was white, just white everywhere. All around him as if he was inside a white ping pong ball. Andrew was also suspended in mid-air. Still unconscious, in the same suit that he was wearing in Jakarta.

Alan, said a voice in his head. He was definitely hallucinating the whole incident or was dead and it was God speaking in his ear. The latter was the more likely one, taking into account the fact that he had faced a tsunami head on. *Is that you? It's Andrew. Are...are we dead?* Alan wasn't sure how his unconscious friend had gained access to his mind, but he didn't know what to do, spoke out aloud.

He began "Whether you're Andrew or not, I have no answer to your question. I don't know if *I'm* alive or not, let alone you. The last thing I remember is a tsunami crashing down on me and (if you are Andrew) you.' Andrew replied, this time he spoke from his mouth, "You were in my head." "You were in mine! Yet, were unconscious this whole time." Alan said, "Is this heaven?" asked Andrew, still looking stunned. "I'm just as clueless and confused as you." Andrew nodded, just as white mist that had appeared from nowhere began swirling in front of them.

The mist formed the vague shape of a reptilian creature and took on a red hue. The animal then took on a more solid form. It had a dragon-like head, the stereotypical long snout with slits for nostrils and cat-like pupils. Its entire body had red armored scales and had four muscular armed with long menacing talons. The chest merged with a long, serpentine body which melted into the mist.

Both Alan and Andrew heard a voice in their heads, supposedly the creature's as it referred to them as 'humans'. It began with a low growl and then a series of dolphin-like clicks, screeches, roars and barks all rolled into one. Finally it settled into a human language and kept switching till it reached English, "Do you understand now?" "Yes." Alan and Andrew said in unison. The creature nodded, or at least that's what the two humans thought it looked like.

Alan and Andrew were pretty tall for humans but they seemed minuscule compared to the massive creature.

"Find me humans. Find me if you want your planet and the rest of your species to survive." it said in a gentle and warm tone. Andrew did not understand what was going on. He had over a hundred questions but his mind wasn't under his control, he didn't know why he was saying it, but asked, "Where do we find you?" "You will find me and the answers you seek in the islands that you are to come to in five of your days…if you are worthy you *will* find me, but be warned humans, enter only through one of the entrances in the wall of stone and leave through the other. Abide by what I have said if you value your lives. You must find me…soon"

None of this made any sense to either of them. After a brief moment, the creature shape shifted again, slowly it seemed to dissolve into the mist and was gone as quickly as it had materialised.

Immediately after it disappeared, the air before them shimmered and an image appeared. They soon realized that it was moving. It showed a city, set along a bay. Fires were raging and the whole city was glowing bright red. Smoke covered the sky above it and powerful winds were blowing massive waves into the city. The voice of the dragon returned, but it was dull and distant, "This is a mere fragment of the destruction that will occur if you fail to come. It will happen, unless you come. For their sake, you must come."

Alan's mind whizzed and he couldn't see anything at all, though he was sure that his eyes were open. Andrew experienced a similar feeling.

Then Alan saw a boy who was walking towards an old, grey, stone house in his mind, somewhat like a video on a screen. Then the boy turned around. His face was familiar, eyes, short hair and there was something about that lopsided grin.

The truth struck Alan like a blow from a sledgehammer. The boy was Andrew, he had somehow gained access into Andrew's memories. Not only that, he could feel a sharp pain in his right knee. He noticed that Andrew had fallen and his leg was hurt in the exact same spot that Alan's knee throbbed.

The scene shifted and he saw Andrew, older now, probably thirteen, going to school with his younger brothers, Jonah and Lucas.

Now he was in a classroom, telling the teacher something. She turned to another boy and took something out of his bag. The anonymous kid clenched his fist and glared at Andrew as he was being scolded. As she turned around, Alan noticed a set of question papers (probably to cheat for an exam he figured) in the teacher's hand.

Again the location changed, this was giving Alan a headache. The same kid, whose bag had the question papers, had cornered Andrew in an alley with a couple of others.

They started beating Andrew and Alan felt his pain…literally.

Several years rushed by like a movie on fast forward and stopped on the day of the freshman orientation of Oxford university in London. He saw himself shaking hands with Andrew. Then again years went by as Alan saw several events in Andrew's life.

He now knew Andrew's deepest secrets and worst fears. It scared him. This complete control and knowledge of someone's life just gave a person so much power over the other.

Just as Alan saw Andrew's memories, Andrew saw Alan's too.

First he saw a boy, wearing a tiny, kid-sized suit. He saw Alan crying and mysteriously knew why. His father hadn't shown up for his fourth birthday. His mother was trying to console him in Scottish, but he knew what she was saying, "Daddy will be here soon Alan, just another day. He's on his flight right now." Alan still sobbed as he cut the birthday cake.

The scene changed and now he saw twelve year old Alan, cooking up a fight between his classmates and smiling at his handiwork. Alan had a natural talent for manipulation, which explained his successful career as a businessman. He had just moved into that school and didn't have many friends and the other kids teased him quite a bit. Due to this, he found joy in using his talents to make his enemies fight each other. This had been only for a few months, by the time which he had several friends. A year later, he even helped his friends by talking them out of fights with others.

Then he saw Alan standing next to a hospital bed. His father was lying on it, with a large bandage on his leg.

Mr Alastor Sawner had been in the military and had taken a bullet to the knee. Alan had told him this several times. Then he had become a political science professor at a university in the U.S just as Alan had graduated from school and joined Oxford where the two of them had become friends.

Finally as years rushed by, Andrew saw the entire meeting Alan had with the investors. What bothered him most was Alan's secret fear that Sheik Halmeer al-Jilani might have been right.

Generally after such an experience, normal people would have cancelled the expedition altogether, but Alan and Andrew would not. If anything, they were even more fired up to unravel its secrets. Then again, it had threatened to destroy their planet which was hard to ignore coming a dragon that could turn into mist and disappear. They had to go, no matter the obstacles or fear. Even if not for them, for the world. Just as they decided this, they fell and hit something solid. It hurt.

Once their vision returned, they saw that they were on a cliff. The bottom half of a lighthouse stood beside them. It took them no more than a second to realize that they were on the cliff, next to the beach where they had been when the tsunami struck.

Andrew got up and walked over to the edge and took a peek. The beach was below them alright, except the fact that it was under twenty feet of swirling sea water.

Alan walked over and almost stumbled off the cliff. This meant that they hadn't imagined it, there had been a tsunami, he had met a red dragon which wanted them to go to the Tenebris Chorés islands and they had seen each other's memories.

Andrew wanted to confirm something, so he asked, "Alan answer this truthfully. Did you eat toothpaste when you were three?" "Yes, but c'mon I was a kid. How do you…" Alan's voice trailed off. As childish as it sounds, this was all the proof they needed, no one had known about this. Both of them now knew for sure that it had happened.

After a while they heard helicopter blades in the distance. As the noise got louder and they noticed the rescue helicopter descending to their location. The two men screamed and waved both their hands in the air. Alan didn't know what promoted him to say it, but he did, "Not a word about what happened to anyone till we reach the islands." "Agreed." said Andrew.

As the helicopter flew towards the airport, Alan and Andrew saw the horrendous scenes below. Several cars, houses and bodies were floating in the water. The airport was far enough inland and was not flooded.

As soon as the helicopter landed, Alan got out and ran towards the terminal, Andrew followed.

He borrowed a mobile phone from a police officer who was a little displeased at first, but was more than happy to oblige when the billionaire stuffed a thousand dollars in his hand.

"Colin," Alan yelled into the phone, "where are you? Come to the airport at once. Also I want to know where Jimmy is. Immediately." Colin's brain took a while to process the questions and commands, "I am at the airport sir, waiting by the jet. Thank goodness that your alive. I'll try and find Mr Van Lee as soon as I can."

The rescue officers escorted the two men to a food store in the airport. After wolfing down a sandwich, Alan had told the officers that Andrew and he had gone to the mansion and had decided to head to the top of the cliff for the view. Then the earthquake had struck and the lighthouse had toppled over, crushing the residence. They had watched the tsunami from the top of the cliff and had been stranded there till the chopper had arrived.

This was a very convincing story and the officers believed it, though Andrew knew otherwise, he kept quite just as they had decided.

After a shower and changing into fresh clothes at the specially reserved suite at the airport, the men were taken to the Learjet that was waiting for them.

Alan and Andrew boarded the plane followed by Colin. This time Andrew repeated the story which Alan had told the officials.

After the flight had taken off, Colin received a call. With a grim expression he informed Alan that Jimmy was dead. He had been found floating in the debris with the limousine. Luckily his investors had survived. Though it wasn't much consolation, it helped a bit. Though it wasn't his fault, Alan blamed himself for his loyal driver's death.

Alan wouldn't let Jimmy's demise be in vain. He would discover what lied in the Chorés no matter what stood in his way. Jimmy's death proved to be the final motivation that Alan needed. He set his sight on the next leg of his quest, Portland.

In reality, the Chorés was being used as bait. The truth was much larger than any human could possibly imagine. When the Sheik had said that Alan was about to meddle with something other worldly, he had been right.

Chapter 3

ASTROPHYSICS 101

It was around 12'o clock when billionaire, Alan Sawner's private Learjet landed at the Portland International airport. The expensive plane taxied off the runway towards a private slot and came to a halt. Inside the fuselage, Alan and his friend and fellow expedition crew member, Andrew Briston unfastened their seat belts and headed towards the exit.

They were followed by Alan's secretary, Colin Miller. According to Colin, his employer had visited his friend's seaside mansion in Jakarta when a tsunami had struck. Luckily, he had been on a high cliff, sightseeing, and was safe when the rescuers found them.

Alan and Andrew shared a secret. They had actually been on the beach when the tsunami had struck the previous day and they had been somehow transported to another dimension where a dragon like creature had told them to find in in the Tenebris Chorés islands. They had already planned an expedition to unravel its secrets before the incident. Even more astonishing was that they had even gained access to each other's memories.

Now they were here in Portland to meet the third expedition crew member, Dr Delton Kraig. A white Scorpio was waiting to pick them up, just outside the plane.

The driver rushed out to open the door for the two businessman. They got in. Andrew started the conversation, "Where are we heading first?" "My hotel, we'll stay there for an hour or so and then we can go attend Dr Kraig's lecture." Alan replied. He was still a little dull, he had instructed his driver to go back to the Soekarna-Hatta international airport in Jakarta while he visited Andrew's mansion. The tsunami had killed the driver on the way and Alan blamed himself for it. If they'd just headed to the airport instead of going to Andrew's mansion, they may have gotten there in time and Jimmy would be alive.

The events of the past twenty-four hours had been extremely tiring and mentally disturbing for both Andrew and Alan.

"Alan, if it's any consolation, even if you didn't come to the mansion, you could never have outrun the tsunami. The flyover to the airport was crushed by the first earthquake. You could never have escaped. Both Jimmy and you would have died." "Thanks for trying Andrew." Alan said but he made an effort to appear lively.

They headed past Broadway street towards Lloyd Centre mall near which 'The Royal Group of Hotels: Portland' was located.

As the car turned left, Alan saw his five star hotel, a tall twenty storied glass structure. They pulled into the driveway and stopped just outside the sliding doors. The floor was white granite. At the centre of the hall was a tall spire that reached up to the top of the building. The walls were glass. The circular black marble reception desk formed a ring around the central spire. The room was circular too with curved white sofas on the sides with glass tables in front of them.

Six elevators lined the side walls. On the first floor were the restaurants. From the second floor onwards, there were twenty-five rooms on each floor. The twentieth floor had only fifteen rooms, but they were luxury class. All of Alan's hotels had the luxury class suites on the highest floor.

Colin had stayed back in the airport to sort out some immigration issues. Alan and Andrew took the elevator to the twentieth floor.

They stepped out and Alan said, "Here, take this and choose any room you like." handing Andrew an electronic key, "Except rooms two-hundred and three and two- hundred and fifteen. Relax, freshen up and meet me by the elevator in about twenty minutes." "Alright." said Andrew and he was gone.

Alan swiped his electronic card and walked into a suite. The room was fit for a king. It had red and gold upholstery. The hall was huge with a sofa and red carpet that lined the floor. The walls were beige with an original Picasso. The living room had a large leather sofa, with a teak wood dining table with chairs that had leather cushions.

There was a forty-eight inch television with a surround sound system. The bedroom had a four poster, king sized bed and a large wardrobe.

The bedroom also had an attached bathroom. Alan took a quick shower and wore a black suit. He went outside where Andrew was already waiting. As he walked, he thought of the dragon. It had said that they would find it if they were worthy. What if they weren't?

"You're late." said Andrew, he was now wearing denim jeans and a red polo neck shirt. "Ready for lunch?" he asked completely ignoring Andrew's first statement about being late.

They took the elevator down. The automated voice announced, "First floor." The two men stepped out. They decided to try Italian and walked into the 'Taste del Italy' restaurant and chose a table at the end of the aisle.

They decided to go with something light, caviar, some akme levian bread and fine wine.

While their food was being plated, Andrew asked, "Are you really planning to attend Delton's lecture? It's so boring sometimes." "Delton's subject for today's lecture might change your opinion." said Alan, "It's a presentation about the secrets of the Tenebris Chorés."

Meanwhile, Delton Kraig prepared for his presentation. There was something special about that particular presentation, Mr Sawner would be meeting him today.

His expedition to the Bermuda triangle had been a grand success, publishing rights, movies, why even a nomination for a Nobel Prize. Now another great opportunity to get some money. Not that he didn't have an urge to discover its secrets too, the fame and fortune were just a bonus that he really wanted.

Delton walked backstage, notes in hand. His assistant informed him that Mr Sawner and Mr Briston had just entered the lecture hall. Alan, he had expected, but Andrew? Delton wasn't due to see him till they reached Germany. Well it didn't matter.

Delton was a little nervous, apart from his friendship with Alan, Mr Sawner was still his employer and he had to reinforce Alan's confidence in him. This lecture gave him the opportunity to do so. He walked onto the stage towards the dais. He placed his papers on the dais and tapped the mike to check that it was working.

Delton began in his most formal voice, "Ladies, gentlemen, friends, how many times has the following question puzzled you? What lies in the Tenebris Chorés islands? Discover the possible answers with me."

"Not bad, he would make a good businessman." Alan said as he watched Delton speak so professionally.

"As you know, just over a year ago, I headed the Bermuda triangle expedition. At first a few of our boats and men went missing, but we forged ahead and solved one of the greatest mysteries that mankind faced.

Countless people discouraged us, told us it was stupidity to meddle with other worldly things, but we were successful.

Several hundred years ago people feared comets, thinking they were omens of ill fate. They feared them because they knew not as to what they were."

It was a good argument. Basically he was saying that people tend to fear what they don't know. Also, it gave a Alan a bit of reassurance. People like the Sheik had said the same about the Bermuda triangle expedition and it had turned out just fine.

Alan looked at Andrew and said, "Well, we definitely hired the right man."

Delton began again, "The Tenebris Chorés island is now the greatest mystery of the world. All puzzles can be solved if one has the key and I believe that I do. Mr Sawner has arranged an expedition to the islands. It is my great honor and privilege to be part of the expedition crew.

We shall set out from the coast of Hong Kong, five days from now.

One must dream first to achieve. Today's presentation shall be based on speculations of the possible causes for the disappearances and unexplained phenomenon in the Tenebris Chorés islands." As he ended this, he spread his arms wide and bowed ever so slightly. There were quite a few claps and nods from the audience.

"My first theory is as follows. There could be a gravitational anomaly in the islands. That is a sudden increase in gravity at certain spots like in the Bermuda triangle. The cause for these anomalies is not completely clear. But as in the triangle they weaken and disappear completely just before reaching the Karman line, the point from where space begins.

Here are my reasons to support my theory. Firstly the triangle and the Chorés islands share similar incidents. We now know the triangle's secret. So I can relate to the similarity of the incidents and come to the conclusion that they may have a similar cause.

Secondly, I attached instruments to measure gravity to a high altitude weather balloon. As it passed over the central island, it detected a slight increase in gravity, slight, but an increase nonetheless.

Such a minor increase in gravity is natural in places all over the world, but as I said, the gravity abruptly weakens at a certain point which is pretty uncommon. Somewhere around thirty thousand feet."

Just as Delton concluded his first theory, a man wearing black trousers and a black hood walked into the hall. Anger welled up within him at the sight of Delton's smiling face. He would pay for what he had done.

There was something in his pocket, made of metal. It was meant for Delton and he would revive it. Delton was responsible for it. He had convinced everyone otherwise, but no, it was him who had taken his friends and brother to their deaths. This went through the anonymous man's mind as Dr Kraig blabbered something about a high concentration of dark matter on the island.

"Thank the heavens. Its over." said Andrew. Alan frowned slightly, "Even a talk about the Tenebris Chorés didn't interest you?" "Talk? More like torture. He's giving a lecture on possibilities when we're going to discover the truth in a matter of days."

Just as Andrew stopped criticizing Delton, Dr Kraig walked over to them and shook their hands. "Did you like my presentation?" Andrew was the first to reply, "Yeah, fantastic." There was obvious sarcasm in his voice but Delton didn't notice and thanked him. "Truly impressive Doctor." said Alan trying to sound as sincere as possible.

As they walked out of the lecture hall, Delton told them to wait by the entrance of the Kraig University of Astrophysics. He had to get his documents and suitcase before they left.

Alan and Andrew walked down the white tiled corridors. The walls were brown in colour. Delton had departed through a door to their right. Andrew told Alan, "I was pretty exited so far, but now that the journey has begun, I'm getting doubtful." Alan was mildly annoyed, "Andrew we have already informed the press, the world is waiting. Imagine what they would say if we hesitate."

"Alan, we can't risk our lives because of a few criticizing journalists."

"Andrew it's more than that."
"What do you mean?"
"You know what I mean."
"What if the dragon's threat wasn't real?"
"We survived a tsunami after facing it head on."
"That doesn't mean we have to risk our lives."
"It's obvious that it has the power to make that threat real."
"You're right. We have to go."

They stepped out and just stood there, watching students walking into Reed college just a block away. Woodstock had become very popular since Delton's college had opened up a year ago.

Andrew turned around and saw Delton walking stiffly away from the college. He pointed it out to Alan and they decided to follow.

Delton was being closely trailed by a man in a black hood. His hand was pressed against the astrophysicist's back. As they turned left to cross the street, Alan couldn't believe what he saw… the man was holding a pistol, pressed against Delton.

"Get the cops." Alan said and bolted after Delton. Andrew wanted to follow but Alan was depending on him to inform the police, so could do nothing for the time being.

Alan followed the man and Delton through the whole of Woodstock.

Finally they walked into a narrow lane. They kept heading further down the lane and Alan would have to start moving if he had to keep up with the men. The only problem was that if he stepped into the lane and the man noticed him, he would have nowhere to hide. The man might even decide shoot him.

The man stopped and Alan leaped away from the mouth of the lane. The man in the black hood whispered something in Delton's ear and he opened a door to his right. After that, he shoved Dr Kraig in.

Alan quickly head to the spot where the two men had been standing a few seconds ago. The door had a glass window on top. He peeped in. He strained to hear what the man was saying. He kept his hood lowered as he spoke, "Kraig, you're responsible for my brother's death and it's about time that you repent." Death? Delton wouldn't kill anyone. Just then he remembered that a few men had died during the Bermuda triangle expedition, maybe this man's brother was one of them.

Alan felt it again…uncertainty. This was happening more and more since his meeting with the Sheik. Why in the world had he invited him for the presentation.

Now that didn't matter, his top priority was to save Delton. His mind raced through several ideas. Part of him wanted to just wait for Andrew to arrive with the police.

There was no time and he had to act fast. He was betting on chance, if the man decided to bring the gun, it was game over. He braved himself and knocked.

Alan almost yelped with satisfaction, the man had left his gun on the table. Alan pressed his back against the side if the wall.

The man peeped out and when he turned right, his vision was filled by a fist flying towards him. Alan had punched him right in the nose. It snapped with a crack that made Alan wince. The man tried to fight back, but the pain blinded him and he missed by quite a bit. Alan performed a well executed jab to his stomach and David crashed to the floor.

Delton could solve several equations simultaneously but the events of the past twenty minutes had been too much to take in.

Delton had walked into his office back at the college where he found David Harrison waiting for him with a gun. David was the brother of Ronald Harrison. Ronald had been part of the Bermuda triangle expedition. He and a few of his men were meant to do a quick check before Delton and the others went further towards the centre of the triangle.

Ronald's boat had sailed over one of the high gravity spots and had been sucked to the bottom of the sea.

After seeing him in the room David had walked Delton out through the back door till they reached the alley. Then he had been pushed into the room that they now were.

"You're the reason that they're dead. You've meddled in matters that were not to be meddled with and it cost them their lives." Delton was afraid but he had to reply, "Your brother and his men knew that there was no guarantee for their safety. They knew damn well where they were going. I hope you do remember that it's a gravitational anomaly and not something supernatural."

Delton noticed a nerve pulsing in David's temple. He turned his gun towards Dr Kraig and began waving it around as he spoke.

Delton barely paid attention to David's dramatic words, he was more concerned that the gun might accidentally go off.

That was when there was a knock on the door. David placed the gun on the table with the barrel pointing in his direction.

He peeped out and stared left and right. Delton heard a crack and a while later, saw David crash to the floor with a bleeding nose. Alan stepped in and said, "Dr Kraig, I suggest that we leave." Delton was more than pleased to do so.

Chapter 4

MOBSTER

Alan and Delton noticed a few large men approaching. It wasn't until they noticed the guns that they were holding that they ran, Delton and Alan expected a bullet to be permanently planted into their heads, but the men hadn't fired. While Instead, they just stood there.

A second before they exited the lane, a van parked right in front of them. They had been herded into exactly the spot that they had wanted. The doors slid open and the two of them were pulled in by some other anonymous characters. The three men who had been following, loaded David into the van too and climbed in.

The van started and drove away in a matter of seconds, as though the incident had never taken place.

It may have looked like an organized and perfectly executed plan, but it wasn't. They had left David's gun in the room and there was blood from his nose on the floor.

These tiny details may not seem like much, but would be enough for the police to realize that something had gone wrong.

The moment Alan and Delton had been kidnapped, their hands had been tied and their mouths gagged.

The two men's eyes were wide with fear. What had they gotten themselves into now? David was probably one of them, as he wasn't tied up or perhaps they had decided to leave it for later, considering that he was unconscious.

Alan couldn't quite recognize where they were. He wanted to ask them who they were and what business they had with them, but the only thing that came through his gag were a few muffled yelps.

Delton shook about violently. One of the men said, "Stop trashing about Dr Kraig. You'll pay for what you did to our families. You took them to their deaths for your fame. And Alan Sawner, are you prepared to take the responsibility for your crew members' lives in the Tenebris Chorés island? How can you sleep peacefully after that expedition, Delton? Now shut up and enjoy what's left of your miserable lives."

As they drove along, Delton was cursing himself for refusing the armed escort he had been offered by the police on account of the incident in New Jersey. A group of men claiming to be relatives of the crew members who had died in the triangle expedition, had tried to kill Delton. The police had offered to post a few men as his personal bodyguards, but Delton had declined. He felt that his privacy would be disturbed when he worked and he simply could not stand it when his work was disturbed. Now he was cursing himself for refusing.

On the way, they stopped at a signal. In the distance, they heard the wail of police sirens. Eventually they got louder. Alan could see the tension in the men's eyes.

The sound kept getting louder until the car came to a halt right next to the van. Alan looked out through the gap between the sliding doors. Andrew was right there, sitting in one of the cars with a worried expression on his face.

Alan couldn't believe his luck. Salvation was right there and they had no means of reaching it.

The signal turned green and the van began moving again. Alan watched as the police van turned right and drove away, probably heading towards the lane where Alan and Andrew had last seen each other.

This gave them a bit of hope. Maybe they would find something to help trace Alan and Delton to where they were. He prayed that they would make it on time.

They eventually reached a warehouse where there were no horns or any other signs of traffic. They had entered a completely desolate place.

The warehouse had been close after a fire in the late nineties. Since then, it had been abandoned until a few years ago. The families of those who had signed up for the Bermuda triangle expedition had been completely dependent on them. After their deaths, their relatives formed a group of thieves, guns for hire and muscle men.

Soon it was obvious that they were really good at their new jobs and had decided to form a mob of their own. Their only common enemy had been Delton, the reason that their brothers, sons and fathers were dead. When Dr Kraig's university had opened in Portland, it had come as an unexpected gift.

Until then, they had been waiting for the opportune moment to strike and it had finally come.

Alan and Delton were then dumped onto the ground.

There was a man waiting for them, dressed in blue jeans, a beige shirt and black leather jacket. It wasn't the best fashion statement, but the gun in his hand made them ignore it.

The man before them clapped, "What a surprise. Not only Delton Kraig, but Alan Sawner too." Their gags were removed, but their hands were still tied.

Alan looked up, sand still sticking to one side of his face. He asked, "What is it you want?" The man replied, "Revenge. You see Delton here..." Alan cut him off by saying, "I heard that guy telling Delton.That wasn't his fault. He had as much of an idea about the triangle at the time as you did." Alan was saying this to support Delton. He wondered whether someone would have to say the same to save him one day, after his own expedition. Hopefully not.

The man's face twisted into a snarl and he kicked Delton who was lying on the floor right in the face. He turned to Alan and said, "I don't think you understand. Let me show you."

Alan was hefted and dragged along behind the man. Delton was still lying on the ground, moaning loudly. They walked around the warehouse. A few tufts of grass grew along the walls and a few tires lay about. There were also several extremely expensive cars which seemed out of the place.

Alan followed the man to a small playground behind the warehouse. A few kids were busy playing. The man called one of them, over.

The kid came running and embraced the man with a loud, "Uncle." The man tapped his shoulder and sent him back. He said to Alan, "You see Sawner? That boy is my nephew. My brother signed up for Kraig's expedition in the hope that it would bring in a little more money. It brought him nothing, but death. The boy lost his father and I began taking care of him. The stories of the others aren't too different."

Alan didn't know what to say. He wasn't even sure whether to hate them for kidnapping them or to pity their losses.

The man turned around and walked, "Of course, we signed a contract which said that Delton wasn't responsible if anyone died. This was just a day before the expedition when they signed this. We hesitated to sign it because of our concern for our relatives. Delton, instead of telling us the truth, reassured us that no one would be harmed. He lied that he knew what was causing the disappearances and that it wasn't dangerous. For the world to believe it, he said, that the journey had to be made. His exact words were, 'It'll be like a picnic.' He promised us, unofficially though, that no one would die."

Alan couldn't believe what he was hearing. Delton would never do that, He turned to the man and said, "I don't believe you. I won't believe you until Delton says it himself."

The man looked at another, standing a few feet away. He walked back in the direction they had come from.

Soon, Delton Kraig was brought before them. Delton had a pretty bad cut near his mouth. Alan ignored the poor condition of his friend. He asked, "Delton did you promise everyone's safety during the Bermuda triangle expedition? Did you lie to them that you knew what was there and that they would be fine?"

"Delton's eyes were full of tears. He said, "Yes I did. Alan you have to understand. I was poor back then and my family was dependent on me." Alan looked at Delton with disbelief. He screamed, "So were theirs."

Delton shook his head wildly and said, "I didn't want to. Situations forced me to Alan. Please…" he begged. All the while the men stood quietly. Delton continued, "What would you have done in my place?"

Before Alan could process that last question, the mystery man interrupted, "Enough. Alan Sawner you are a good man. Leave now if you want to, cancel the expedition. That will save lives, but I'm afraid, Delton dies here."

Alan couldn't help, but feel that the man was right. Was the dragon's threat even genuine?

He turned to the man and said, "As appealing as it sounds, I cannot cancel the expedition. It is too important. I can't tell you why, but I have to go to the island and Delton is coming with me." Though Alan said this pretty heroically, he had no idea how he might escape from here.

The man sighed and turned around. Two men seized Alan and Delton by the arms and took them into the warehouse through a side gate.

The inside was larger than they had expected. It was filled with old boxes and other goods.

Alan and Delton were made to kneel. Immediately they knew what was going to happened. They were to be shot.

They heard the man's voice from behind them. He was saying, "Alan you still have a chance, cancel the expedition, leave Delton and go." Alan didn't speak.

They heard the click of a gun being loaded. Then there was a loud, unmistakeable, crack of a gun being fired. One of the men who was about to shoot Alan crashed to the floor. Both Alan and Delton turned around.

It was that moment that the S.W.A.T team chose to break in. The men entered with their guns raised and the whole place turned in to a war zone.

A bullet fired by one of the men hit a sinister looking box which immediately erupted into flames. The fire alarm, which the men had installed, began buzzing. Guns were firing, fires were blazing and alarms were wailing.

Alan and Delton ran, their arms still tied. One of the men from the assault team noticed them and ran to help. On his way the poor officer was blown up by a grenade.

The team who had been ordered not to kill, were shooting at the men's arms and legs only incapacitating them and on the whole were having a really tough time. The mobsters on the other hand were firing carelessly, setting off more fires.

Alan eventually found a sharp edge on a metal box which he used to cut his bonds free. He then helped Delton and the men ran towards the exit.

Their path was blocked by the same man who had explained everything to Alan earlier. He raised his gun and the two others raised their hands. Alan doubted he would accept their surrender.

He was then shot in the shoulder by a S.W.A.T member. He fell to the ground, but was still alive.

They ran out of the warehouse and onto the lane. They knew that their former captors were more than occupied, but kept running as fast as they could.

Just then Alan and Delton's path was blocked by the Man's nephew who they had seen earlier in the playground.

He said, tears streaming down his cheeks, "You're the reason my uncle Alan is dead."

So that man's name was Alan too and now the boy thought he was dead. This made Alan Sawner feel a mixture of emotions. It was a feeling that can't be explained with words.

The boy had seen his uncle being shot and had probably assumed that he was dead. Delton said, "He's alive. The bullet hit him in the arm." This sentence made no sense to the young boy. According to him, this man was the reason he had lost his the last of his family.

He picked up a stone and threw it at Delton which hit him square in the chest. Then he seemed to realize something and took something out of his pocket. It was a gun.

His arms sagged due to his weight, but he held it up as high as he could.

Alan and Delton ran. The boy fired a few shots, but none of them reached their mark. The kid eventually ran out of bullets and couldn't catch up with the men.

He crashed to the floor and began howling in sorrow.

Alan stopped. He couldn't just leave him crying on the street. Delton on the other hand was a little less concerned. He wanted to get out of their as soon as possible. He held Alan by the arm and began dragging him away from there.

Just as they stepped out of the lane, Andrew rushed towards them with a squadron of policemen. "They're in there. The S.W.A.T may need some help" said Alan pointing down the alley with a thumb. The policemen ran in with their guns raised.

They got in with the commander and headed to a branch of the Lifecare hospitals.

While Delton was being treated, Alan told Andrew everything that had happened. Andrew asked, "Andrew, do you think Delton is a good person?" Andrew replied, "Well Alan, circumstances can change even the best of people." Alan still wasn't convinced. He said, "But those people…how could he have done that to them and that boy. We just left him there."

Andrew was having a tough time convincing his friend that it wasn't his fault done anything wrong.

They were then taken to a local police station where they were debriefed. Delton told them what had happened, leaving a few parts out, but was having a tough time explaining it.

Alan was next. He's left out the part where the kid had drawn a gun on them. He didn't want to make the kid's life any worse.

Later, he decided that he would arrange for the boy to have a better life. How he would do it was still a bit of a puzzle

It took an hour to clear things up and they were finally allowed to leave.

The same Scorpio was waiting for them. They climbed in and headed towards the international airport. Everyone's mind pondered over the same thing. Would someone have to die to reveal the secrets of the Tenebris Chorés?

The car drove directly to the Learjet that had flown Alan and Andrew over from Jakarta (perks of being a billionaire). They were greeted by Colin who was a big fan of Delton's.

After the immigration was done and the flight got clearance, it rolled off the runway and started ascending, flying at five hundred miles per hour towards New York.

Chapter 5

GATEWAY

It was 2:00 am. Patrick Maple was still awake, standing in the great lawn, central park, Manhattan. Many may wonder what he was doing there, but he had permission from the mayor himself. Patrick was conducting an experiment. He had got the required documents signed in a couple of hours. Who would deny a Nobel prize winning geologist? Actually quite a few people, but Patrick preferred not to think so. His arrogance would prove to be his downfall.

His digital watch that his brother Alex had gifted him beeped. It meant that it was time to head back to his home. Half an hour, that's all he needed, but that would mean being late. He cursed under his breath and hoisted the seismic sensor out of the ground.

He would take a cab to his bungalow on Lexington Avenue. He walked onto the main road. A familiar yellow New York cab drove towards him. Patrick outstretched his right hand and yelled, "Taxi."

A brown BMW was driving three VIPs from the LaGuardia airport. Their flight had been grounded for several hours in Chicago due to hazardous weather conditions and powerful wind shears. It was almost 1:30am when they reached New York.

Alan Sawner was one of them. The billionaire's expedition to the mysterious Tenebris Chorés islands had made the front page of every newspaper in the world. It was due in four days. The world's news channels were already discussing the outcomes of the expedition. The world's attention was focused on them.

The other passengers of the car were Mr Andrew Briston and Dr Delton Kraig.

Mr Briston too was a businessman. He was Alan's close friend and part of the island expedition crew.

Dr Delton Kraig was the most famous astrophysicist in the world and had been the chief scientist of the Bermuda Triangle expedition. Who better than Dr Kraig to be the third member of the Tenebris Chorés expedition?

The East river shined below them in the moonlight as they drove over the Robert F. Kennedy bridge towards Manhattan.

Alan felt that 'the city that never sleeps' was an apt title for New York. Even at that late hour there was quite some traffic.

Patrick had just gotten out of the cab and paid the driver when his phone rang, "Hello?"

> "Mr Maple please be ready to leave in ten minutes."
> "Mr Sawner?"
> "Yes it's me."
> "Is Dr Kraig with you?"
> "Yes and Andrew too. Please hurry up."
> "Goodbye."
> "See you in a while."

Andrew and Patrick got along well, but Delton. He couldn't stand the sight of him. An overgrown baby. Yes that's what Kraig looked like. Or at least, that was what Patrick liked to think.

The main door had a mat which said 'welcome'. The was a triangular covering jutting out from above the main door. It was held up by two Greek style columns.

The main hall had maple wood flooring (Patrick Maple's way of humor). There was a white sofa in the corner. There was a showcase against the wall. It was lined with several trophies. The other walls were lined with photographs of Patrick receiving various awards. His most prized possession was the picture of himself receiving the Nobel prize.

Patrick decided to take the Nobel prize photograph with him. He took it off the wall and went upstairs to his room.

The bedroom had a queen sized bed. There were two lamps placed on shelves on either side of the bed. Patrick had already packed his clothes for the trip to save time.

Patrick opened his wardrobe and took out a briefcase. It had his clothes, a few documents and also some geological records. He placed the photograph in the briefcase and closed the wardrobe. He looked at himself in the mirror and smiled. A handsome man stared back. His life would be perfect, if it wasn't for Delton. His idea would lead to the colonisation of a planet. Yet Delton's stupid expedition had overshadowed him.

A couple of years ago Patrick was the most popular scientist in the world. Until Delton had popped up from nowhere with his idea to send an expedition to the Bermuda triangle.

Patrick had started the process of colonizing Mars and the world had forgotten him. Patrick had lost his title of the most popular scientist in the world to some second rate astrophysicist. He was still extremely popular as a geologist, but it didn't matter to Patrick, someone had beaten him and he would beat that person back. Alan's expedition had gotten him fired up. If he discovered the cause of the disappearances before Delton, that would be the ultimate insult.

Patrick saw a car pull up in front of his house. The geologist knew exactly who it was. The car honked as Patrick switched off the lights.

He typed in a four digit security code and slammed the door shut behind him. The door was a self-locking version, so Patrick didn't have to bother locking it with his key. He ran to the car and got in.

The car drove away, back towards the airport. No one could have possibly predicted that the owner of that house would never walk through those doors again.

They took the same route back to the airport. Though it was almost winter, it had started raining on the way. Visibility was very low and it took them quite a while to reach the airport.

The rain had worsened, several flights including their private plane had not gotten clearance to take off. They would have to wait till the rain died down. They were escorted to a private waiting room and told to make themselves feel at home.

"Well, what do we do now?" asked Alan. "The only thing we *can* do is wait." Delton had a question at the back of his mind and by the looks of thing, they would have to stay here for quite a while. So he decided to ask, "Alan, the events of the past two days. The obstacles that we're facing…they seem like a warning."

Patrick didn't want to let slip even the slightest opportunity to argue with Delton and win. "Dr Kraig, are you suggesting that there is something supernatural in the islands that doesn't want us going there? I feel that the stress and pressure of our upcoming expedition has gotten to you. Maybe you should rest and prepare yourself for the *next* expedition and leave this one to us." Patrick's voice was layered with concern, concealing the venom within.

Delton didn't know what Mr Maple had against him. They weren't even of the same profession, he was an astrophysicist and Patrick was a geologist. "I am not suggesting supernatural causes for the disappearances. I am merely saying that sometimes, bad things form a chain reaction. Sometimes there are warnings that we must understand."

Andrew's mind was even more confused after hearing what the two scientists were saying. Maybe Delton was right and there was a reason behind the setbacks, but he felt different. They would find the dragon in the Chorés islands if they were worthy. "Maybe this is a test." he said out loud and almost clasped his mouth shut with his hands when he finished.

Everyone stared at him. Luckily Alan came to his rescue, "Do you mean fate is testing us? You aren't going into philosophy, are you?" Andrew didn't mind making himself look stupid to shield the truth from the others and said, "It was just a thought."

That was a close one. Alan looked at Andrew and his expression said, 'Its okay.' He was grateful to Alan for the save.

"Let's watch some television. To get our minds off things." They turned to BBC and their jaws fell open in awe at the video being played. It showed a flare erupting from the central island. A column of flame extended into the sky.

"Yes!" exclaimed Patrick. None of the other occupants of the room could comprehend how an inferno erupting from the island which they were to visit could possibly be good.

"Yes?" asked Delton. Patrick was pleased that the question had come from Delton. He had eagerly waited for something to happened, a disappearance, anything at all. A lose of one life was a necessary sacrifice but this had been incredible. No one had died, but he had got his event.

Patrick began a well rehearsed explanation, "My friends, I have planted several seismographs on the outer islands of the Tenebris Chorés. They have been recording the seismic activity of the islands for a few weeks now. I also recorded the seismic activity of Central Park, a location with the regular seismic activity of any other place in the world. If the reason behind the happenings on that island is geological, there will be a change in seismic activity during any event. This will be recorded by my equipment. My friend's lab in Brooklyn has the data of both places. If we compare it, we may unravel the secrets of the Chorés right here from New York."

Delton ran to the entrance of the room and said, "What are we waiting for? Let's go." Alan and Andrew got up and followed. Patrick was the last to leave the room. Delton's excitement had been genuine, but Patrick was sure that he was doing it just to mock him.

They told the manager that they would be back soon and got into the car. Alan decided to drive. Andrew sat next to him in front. Patrick was forced to sit next to Delton. He would have protested on any other occasion but he was too engrossed in making some calculations. He often yeller random things like, "Five hundred and eighty multiplied by nine hundred and thirty-five." They sped over Brooklyn bridge towards Marcus Shaw's lab on Atlantic avenue.

Patrick told Alan to park in front a pale grey building that could have been anything, a movie theatre, apartments or even a factory. The truth was that it belonged to a geologist named Marcus Shaw. It was a state of the art laboratory which had the best of technology.

The four of them got our of the car though it was still raining. They entered a white corridor through reinforced steel doors. They reached a pair of beige doors like the ones found in hospitals. As they entered, they saw a man, probably in his late sixties with grey hair leaning on a steel table. He was staring into a number monitors.

Marcus Shaw barely noticed the four people who had walked into his lab. "Marcus, show me the reading." said Patrick, without even sparing a second for a 'hello'. Marcus didn't seem to mind. He turned the monitor towards Patrick with slim fingers.

Patrick turned a keyboard towards him and typed in some commands. Immediately the window which played the video of the flare minimized and several graphs and charts popped up. The other expedition crew members stood aside and watched. "Marcus, don't just stand there, help me." Dr Shaw shrugged and walked over to a different computer.

Patrick's lips curled and his joy became more obvious. He pressed 'enter' and waited eagerly. A processing bar appeared on the screen. Two words were now displayed on the screen, 'Match Found'. Patrick's hands shot up in the air, almost punching Marcus.

Alan and the group were completely clueless. Andrew began, "What happened?" Patrick was too excited to answer. He took a few deep breaths to calm himself down and said, "I had a theory that the central island could be a sort of gateway."

A gateway? What was Patrick talking about? "Mr Maple, are you suggesting that the island could be a gateway in the sense, a bridge between dimensions. A wormhole maybe?" If only he was in possession of a gun, Patrick would have shot Delton then and there. "No Doctor, I am saying that it could be a geological gateway. That is, a gateway to a network of tunnels throughout the world. The central island and its surround areas may be the weak spots, where the land or ocean floor is thin enough to cave in. Dragging boats and people down into the tunnels. Now one may point out that this theory does not explain the missing planes but they may not take into consideration that where the land is thin, though it has not been proved, the magnetism emanating from the metallic core of the earth may be stronger, causing navigational equipment to malfunction, resulting in plane crashes. It is true that not a single geologist has agreed with me, but I have my reasons which I will reveal later."

Alan nodded, though it didn't explain the dragon, nothing did, but it made sense to some extent. Delton decided that it was about time he stopped taking Patrick's irritating retorts. Dr Kraig was not a geologist, but he knew something about the subject. So he asked, "Still, there is one thing that puzzles me. How could the earth's magnetism be amplified to such an extent?"

Patrick had been waiting for someone to ask that question. He was almost happy that Delton had posed the question though Patrick disliked him. On second thought, maybe someone else should have asked him that. He said, "I recreated these conditions on a smaller scale in my lab and it works out. If scaled up, they would be just enough to cause the equipment onboard the plane to malfunction. Though this sounds crazy, I assure you, it's true."

Patrick Maple started again in a matter-if-fact like voice, "Also what many people don't know is that these flares are regular under the earth's crust. These tunnels could lead far below the earth, allowing these flares to escape. My theory is that it formed somewhere else in a different tunnel and traveled to the weak spots under the central island finally breaking through." Delton was starting to dislike Patrick for his mannerism but he had to appreciate the theory.

Mr Maple wasn't done yet, "I ran some simulations earlier. The data that the seismographs picked up during the flare matched with my simulations. Thus adding more matter to my theory. Alas these seismographs were not on the main island. I have to be on sight to confirm it."

Delton ignored Patrick for a while and looked at the screen. For a fraction of a second he saw something in the flare. He walked closer to the monitor and played the video. Again he saw it and pressed the pause button.

Dr Delton Kraig was baffled. "There's a dragon in the flare." he said. When Delton's words reached his ear, Patrick was sure that the astrophysicist had lost it. True that he had mocked him of going mad but this was crazy. "Dr Kraig have you..." Patrick wanted to speak but his mouth wouldn't obey. There was an actual dragon like being in the flare.

Alan and Andrew were the first to react to Delton's statement. "Rocks." said Andrew. "What?" asked Delton. Alan grasped what Andrew meant and added to it, "Patrick, if that flare came from underground, it is possible that there could have been rocks in it?" Patrick recovered from the shock and thought for a second before speaking, "Well any rock should have melted but if the flare had broken through a layer of rock instead of a preformed opening...it is possible." "It's settled then. The only way we're going to discover the truth is by going to the island in person." Andrew concluded.

The rain had subsided and their jet could now take off. Alan got a call from the airport manager, giving them the good news. They said their goodbyes to Marcus and exited the building. Patrick was last to leave. Just before stepping onto the pavement, he whispered something in Marcus's ear. The old man nodded and Mr Maple boarded the car.

As they drove back to LaGuardia airport, Alan and Andrew thought back to the dragon they saw in the flare. Everyone was now convinced that it was a large rock, except Alan and Andrew who knew the truth. They knew exactly what it was...more or less.

Once they reached, they were taken directly to the plane where they were welcomed by Colin. He shook hands with Alan and told him that he would see them the day after in Hong Kong. Their luggage had been brought from the waiting lounge in which they had been earlier.

The jet took off again. Taking yet another expedition member towards a different destination. Alan said as they flew over the Atlantic, "Paris, here we come."

Chapter 6

HAUNTING WORDS

It was 8:00am in Paris. The Paris-Charles De Gaulle airport was filled with tourists. The airport was awaiting a special arrival. The controller gave a white Learjet clearance for its final approach. Anxious journalists watched as the plane taxied towards its specially reserved apron and came to a halt.

Four very important individuals got down. First to disembark was a tall man with dark hair and chocolate brown eyes in a designer suit. He waved a hand. His smiling face masked the anxiety within.

Any experienced psychologists would deduce that this man showed high levels of confidence and the traits of a leader in his body language. This was none other than Alan Sawner.

Even a five year old would recognise Alan's face from the newspapers and television channels due to his expedition to the eerie and mysterious Tenebris Chorés islands.

The next to set foot onto the asphalt was an equally prominent gentleman, Andrew Briston. Alan's college time friend and fellow expedition member was dressed in a silk polo neck shirt and grey trousers.

Andrew and Alan knew something which they had sworn not to reveal to the other crew member until they reached the island.

This secret was the meeting they had with a mysterious dragon-like creature in Jakarta. They had been on a beach when the third largest tsunami ever recorded had struck the coast. Yet they had miraculously survived. The dragon had said that they would find it and the answers to their questions if they were worthy. If they could survive the trials that the island held in store for them, they would definitely be the worthiest humans on planet Earth.

The other two passengers of the plane were Dr Delton Kraig and Mr Patrick Maple.

Delton was the world's leading astrophysicist. His greatest achievement was discovering the secret behind the Bermuda triangle disappearances (at the cost of a few lives).

Patrick was the greatest geologist of all time. His scheme to colonise Mars was a truly humongous step in the history of mankind. To colonise another planet...incredible!

Just a day after Patrick's automated col-bots (colonisation robots) had started recreating Mars's atmosphere, Delton had come up with his expedition and stolen the world's attention. Patrick had become old news and Delton had become a star.

The only two occasions that Patrick had surfaced in the news was when he launched a calculated nuke to kick-start the resurrection of Mars's magnetic field and the time that he had received a Nobel prize for his project.

Patrick loathed Delton for stealing his spot as the most famous scientist (in general) in the world. Patrick held the second spot and still earned millions. Immature indeed, but when it comes to competitions, even adults tend to act childish.

This was Patrick's big chance to regain his status. If he unravelled the island's mystery before Delton, the world would know him again. Not that they already didn't. In fact countless people admired him. Alas, Patrick's arrogance wouldn't allow him to be satisfied with the attention of the entire galaxy.

Alan, Andrew, Delton and Patrick were greeted my charging journalists. A flurry of questions followed.

"Any comment on the flare yesterday?"
"Are you still going to proceed?"
"What do Miss Frost and Mr Maple say?"
"What is your plan now Mr Sawner?"
"How long will you stay in Paris?"
"Are you scared?"

Alan and company squeezed through, answering any question they could decipher through the noise. Finally they boarded a Land Rover and drove out of the terminal.

"Where is Martha's lab by the way?" asked Patrick. Andrew answered, "Not too at from here. Its on Rue Ronsard." Patrick nodded and they travelled in silence. Everyone was under a lot of pressure. The constant travel and stressful thoughts had taken its toll on the men. A day's break was exactly what they needed.

The traffic was moderate and it took the troop approximately twenty minutes to reach Martha's lab/greenhouse. The structure was really impressive. It was a glass dome with a projected entrance. The door was a reinforced aluminium alloy. One may point out that a thief could just break the glass and the door wouldn't be of much use, but what that person may not realize was that the glass was just under a metre thick and had a custom designed alarm system wired into it. Even Houdini might not have been able to escape the lab if he was locked inside.

They walked over to the door and Delton spoke into the intercom, "Miss Frost it's Dr Kraig, we're here."

The lot of them were no older than twenty-four and hated being formal. They had been dumped with more a hundred times more responsibilities than the usual rookie out of college. Maybe it's true that people do well under pressure.

Martha buzzed them in and the crew entered. The jutting passageway was pretty plain with nothing more than a tiled floor and potted plants on either side.

The dome was a completely different set up. It was literally a miniature jungle. The centre of the circular dome had a massive glass box. The box was further divided into four. Each of these boxes had an entrance and held a variety of tress, shrubs, bushes and wildlife. The dome was larger than it appeared from the outside. Each box had a different variety of plant and animal life. The lab gave Delton the creeps. He could have sworn that he saw at least twelve snakes in one of the boxes.

Martha Frost walked around the curve of the wall, wearing a suit beneath a lab coat. Her eyes were covered with protective goggles and her blonde hair was tied behind in a ponytail. The four newcomers to the lab shook her gloved hand, greeting her in turn.

Alan was the first to speak, "Hello Martha, it gives me great joy in knowing that you will accompany us. We need to get as much information of the place as possible. That includes knowledge of the island's vegetation and wildlife." Martha tried her best to conceal her excitement but was doing a poor job. No one blamed her, they were all pretty tensed. Who wouldn't be? After all they were about to make a journey to an islands from where no one had returned. Anyone who went close either had crazy hallucinations or went completely insane.

Martha had indulged herself in her work to get her mind off the expedition, but the sight of her the crew had brought the anxiety and tension back up. Eager to change the topic, she said, "Well, before we get on about the Tenebris Chorés, I would like to show you my latest piece of work."

After that statement, Martha walked over to a table which none of them had noticed and lifted what looked like a hypodermic syringe, except it was made of metal and had a digital display panel. "This device can analyse the cell structure of plants and animals to determine which family they belong to." explained Martha. "For example, a lion and a cat being of the same family. Its database can trace a species back to the cretaceous period. One of Alex's inventions." There were a few occasions when Patrick felt jealous of his own brother. This was one of them. Alex invented this and Alex invented that. How irritating.

Alan knew that they had another day to go, but felt that there was no point in standing here and talking about plants. He began, "Not to be rude Martha, but we should get moving now. Have you got your things?" Martha was a bit taken aback by Alan's interruption but quickly recovered and said, "Sorry Alan, I just got a bit too involved in explaining the device's usefulness in this expedition. Yes I'm ready, we can leave." She grabbed a suitcase from the table which they had also failed to notice.

They took the same Land Rover. Alan decided to drive and sent the driver away. Andrew sat next to him. Delton and Martha were behind the two businessmen. Patrick sat alone at the back, silently thinking, *This is the last time you put me behind you Delton.* With this childish thought they drove off towards 'The Royal Group of Hotels: Paris'

The hotel was on Rue Villedo. It towered above the smaller buildings, a massive steel and glass structure seemed to glow as it reflected the sunlight. The Paris branch was one of the largest of Alan's hotels.

The driveway curved around a statue of some Greek god. It was covered by a dome, held up by six columns.

The former four, now five passengers of the car climbed up the dark marble stairs and into the hotel through sliding glass doors. Alan and company were greeted to a series of 'oohs' from the tourists. Those who weren't so surprised ran towards them to shake their hands. Some nerdy kid with glasses even asked Delton for an autograph. Patrick swore under his breath but kept a decent look on his face.

Alan felt a hand close around his forearm and was dragged out of the crowd. He was surprised to see Montres Phillepe. *"Bonjour* Alan. Having a nice time I presume." Alan knew that Montres lived in Paris but he hadn't expected to run into him. "Hello Montres. I wasn't expecting to see one of my investors here." Montres let out a laugh and said, "Well I do live in Paris. It is a big city and bumping into you would have been quite a coincidence, but this isn't one. I came to invite you to my little celebration today. On account of my investment in your expedition. It will be great to have the other expedition members there too." Alan considered for a while and said, "I would be glad to attend, but I must speak to the others too. I'll inform you in about an hour." "Sure. Take your time." with this last sentence, Montres walked away.

Alan and the rest of the group went to one of the many restaurants. "Montres has invited us to a party this evening." Andrew sighed and said, "It's clearly a publicity stunt. Having all the expedition members attending *his* party."

The group hesitated a bit at first, but agreed to go. Patrick on the other hand excused himself by claiming to be ill. The truth was slightly more sinister than that. He was waiting for a package from a geologist, his friend, Marcus Shaw.

Patrick's brother, Alex, was too busy with preparing their equipment and so couldn't go. It was just going to be Alan, Andrew, Delton and Martha. Alan made the call to Montres and told him. "I am delighted," he had said, "but it is unfortunate that the Maples won't be able make it. I shall expect your arrival in the banquet hall at 8'o clock this evening." *A party may be just the thing to get it out of my head,* thought Alan. By *it,* Alan was referring to his confusion regarding the incident in Jakarta.

Alan and company headed to the banquet hall on the thirtieth floor that evening. They were welcomed by Montres, "Always a pleasure Alan. Greetings to you too Andrew, Martha and Delton. I see that you are on time." Andrew replied as he shook Montres's hand, "It's better than being late at least."

The crowd piled in soon enough. As they walked on, Alan noticed a familiar face and his heart sank. His first thought was, *Not him again.* The face belonged to Sheik Halmeer al-Jilani.

Andrew had shared Alan's memories when they had met the dragon and he knew why his friend was so disturbed at the sight of that man. As though on cue, the man walked towards them with a broad smile on his face.

"Mr Sawner, how are you?" beamed the Sheik. Alan swallowed, forced his lips into a smile and replied, "I'm doing great Sheik Halmeer. Truly a pleasant surprise to see you here."

The Sheik's expression changed and he said, "Did you consider of what I said in Jakarta." The truth was that Alan thought about it almost every five minutes but he said, "Well Sheik Halmeer, I gave you my reply right there and I for one am very firm in my decisions. Why would I have to reconsider?" The Sheik sighed in an almost sympathetic manner, "Well Alan…I still think that the island is a place that are to be left alone by mankind." Alan kept a peaceful expression, but those words haunted him every second. The biggest question in his mind was: *Will this venture lead to discoveries or death?*

Andrew had been watching from afar and saw Alan clearly struggling not to yell at the Sheik to shut up. He decided to help and called out to Alan. His friend was glad for the rescue and politely excused himself.

An hour after the crew had arrived, the last of the guests entered the hall and Montres took the stage. "Ladies and gentlemen," he began. "I would like to thank you all for coming. Today we have some special guests here. Alan, Andrew, Delton and Martha…the stage is yours."

Naturally the other three allowed Alan to speak. After all the whole expedition was his. He stepped onto the dais and said, "Good evening everyone. I have just one thing to do. I wish to think my good friend Montres and of course all my other investors. This expedition is sure to unravel countless secrets and bring answers to various questions. I promise that we will put all our efforts into discovering the truth behind the Chorés. Well I must take your leave now. We'll see you the day after in Hong Kong at the press meet. Thank you." There was a round of applause. It was a fairly good speech considering the fact that Alan hadn't expected to be delivering one.

The rest of the party was pretty much the usual. There was a vegetarian and a non-vegetarian section. A few guests danced and some others had either champagne or wine.

At around 10'o clock the expedition members went back to their rooms. Before sleeping Alan and Andrew thought for the sake of sanity, *What the Sheik said was just nonsense. The dragon was a figment of our imagination.* With this calming thought they began dreaming of two dragons, similar to structure as the one they had seen, fighting with two large staffs above an ocean of lava. Not quite the peaceful slumber they had expected.

The scene changed and Alan saw himself standing on a hill. There were no tress but plenty of grass. There was a guy in what appeared to be a pirate's costume. There was an age old pistol in a holster on his belt. He also had a sword. Another person was next to him, wearing glittering purple robes. This individual also had five rings on his right hand. Each one with a different coloured stone.

There was something about that scene though, something that disturbed Alan. He concentrated on their faces and was shocked to find that they all had the same face, his face.

The next morning was rather uneventful. Their flight to Hong Kong was scheduled that evening. Alan met the others at the restaurant that they had decided the previous day.

Alan's friends were sitting at the fifth table from the left in the luxury end. He was dressed in one of his brown, designer suits that matched his eyes. Delton waved him over with a grin and for some reason Alan felt that Patrick had rolled his eyeballs or it could have just been the lighting.

"Good morning Alan." said Martha. "Good morning to you too. Did anyone contact Alex yet?" said Alan. Patrick set down his fork and said, "Yeah, I did. He's ready, except that he has to sign some papers regarding the arrival of our transport on the island."

The group decided to do whatever they wished to, until lunch time when they would leave for Alex's place. Andrew's exact words were, "You have the rest of the day to yourself. Meet back at the hotel lobby at three. I would recommend finishing lunch as we've got a long journey ahead to Alex's residence."

The rest of the day was enjoyed differently by each of the members. Alan preferred to stay at the hotel and listen to music the whole time. Andrew and Delton headed to the gaming room for a face-off. Patrick choose a peaceful swim. Martha opted for a visit to the Eiffel tower. Before they knew it, the time had come to leave.

They had all finished lunch at one of the hotel's restaurants and assembled at the lobby. The employees had loaded their luggage into the Land Rover and they left for Alex's house.

It had taken them over two hours to reach since they had left the hotel. Patrick was driving and parked in front of an extravagantly built white bungalow. The gates swing open automatically and a beep sounded. Though none of them were aware of it, the beep signified the disabling of the alarm system. If it had been on, they would have been falling through a tunnel which had seemingly appeared from nowhere, that led to a chamber where they would have been netted and subdued with a special gas to make them unconscious till the police arrived. This could definitely be certified as paranoia but Alex's inventions were too precious to be lost or worse, stolen.

Alex appeared at the doorway and raised a hand. He said as he walked towards them, dragging his suitcase behind him, "Hello everyone. I'm packed and ready to leave." Some of you may consider it rude not to invite the group in for tea, but time was short and they had to hurry up. They exchanged a few words and turned around towards the car. Out of curiosity, Delton asked, "Hey, Alex, what's our transport anyway?" Alex was happy to break the awkward silence, "Its a camper." Andrew didn't think he heard him right, "I don't think I heard you right. Did you say a camper?" Alex nodded, "Yes, a camper. Its armour plated and has modifications that you won't find in any run of the mill family picnic vehicle." No one objected. They all knew of Alex's capabilities.

The next one and a half hours were spent navigating through the ever increasing traffic and pondering about the expedition ahead.

As usual, the car drove straight to the plane. This one belonged to Andrew. Not to forget that he was an equally successful businessman too. What no one else knew was that Andrew had been a hidden investor. His funds had replaced the Sheik's since they had run into a minor financial shortage.

The plane was just being refuelled as they boarded. One of Andrew's employees loaded the luggage. A few minutes for them to get clearance and the plane taxied onto the runway.

One thing was sure though, the stage was set and the true journey, that would decide the fate of the world, was about to begin.

Chapter 7

PHOTO PLEASE

William Silver was having a tough time sleeping. Tomorrow he was going to get a chance to speak to Alan Sawner. His school had thrown in a few thousands as a donation for his expedition in return for some publicity. William had been chosen to ask the billionaire a few questions. It was going to be live and the world would obviously be watching. He forced himself to calm down and being a logical person, decided that he would need his concentration. He slept, hoping that his question would be good enough.

Alan Sawner had had a relatively peaceful sleep. He had been aroused from his sleep only once when they had landed in Dubai to refuel. It was early morning when they reached Hong Kong. There was tension in the air. It was as though the world was holding its breath.

The entire group were wearing suits except Martha who was in a green dress. The plane was about to land in a few minutes and they were all seated. Patrick was first to speak, "You wait for it all these months and when it finally comes, you feel terrified." Nobody replied. Alan tried to divert himself by looking at the clouds outside. His mind revolved around what the Sheik had said. In reality it wasn't just the Sheik, it had been the hundreds of people that Alan had met for the past six months. The incident with the dragon had caused those memories to surface. So many had warned him against going there. Was it the right choice? He would know by the end of that day.

The plane landed at the Hong Kong international airport. The crew finally had all its six members, Alan, Andrew, Delton, Patrick, Martha and Alex. Each leg of their journey up to that point had just been travel with barely any action, except when Delton had been kidnapped. It was similar to going from sleeping to running a marathon in a matter of seconds.

As they stepped onto the ground, they felt like they had entered a battlefield. They were an army facing off against a fierce monster that had taken the shape of an island.

The sight of a friendly face comforted Alan. It was Colin Miller, Alan's secretary. The individuals shook Colin's hand as he said, "How are you gentlemen, madam, I hope you are ready?" "We are doing just fine, unless you take into account the nervousness. Anyway we're as ready as we'll ever be."

Colin walked aside with Alan to tell him the plans, "Mr Sawner, we will soon be heading to attend a private conference with the investors, some distance from Tai O. The press conference is at 10'o clock at the Tai O public pier. Then there's that student talk show. After all this we'll be finishing lunch and you shall head off from there to the fourth island and then central one." The last sentence hung in the air for a while. Alan called the others over and they joined the billionaire and his secretary.

Alan had been burdened with his business at a young age and had few friends. The expedition members were the only thing he had close enough to call buddies. He hoped that nothing bad would happen to them. Alan's mother would be there too. For some reason, the thought of her made him feel like abandoning the expedition and going home. He might die out there. If he did, his mother might… Her husband had passed away five years ago and her son was all that she had. What if Alan and the group never returned? What if the other five died with him? How might their families feel? Could Alan bear this tremendous burden? These were just a few of the countless questions that whizzed through Alan mind as he drove towards the conference.

It took the two cars approximately forty-five minutes to reach the location. Alan, Andrew and Patrick had gone in one, leaving Martha, Delton and Alex to come behind them in the second one. *Now whose behind, huh?*, thought Patrick.

They stopped in front of a glass column that dwarfed its neighbours. It was basically occupied by the offices of several companies. The thirtieth floor belonged to Mr Lai Chee Yen, one of Alan's investors. This was where the conference was going to be held

The reaction of the people once they entered was similar to how they might react to a film star. They surged towards the rather startled group like an army. Alex unconsciously took a step back. It took a few minutes for the crowd to stop asking them questions and taking photos.

Some critics had claimed the whole expedition to be a publicity stunt. Though it wasn't, it worked pretty well as one.

The crew took the elevator to the respective floor. They were welcomed by an unsmiling guard wearing a navy blue uniform. They followed Mr Grumpy to a circular room with glass on one side. The man left. There were a few more entrances through which the rest of the other investors piled in and took their seats at a long table. The guard gestured for them to sit down and they did. He then turned around and left.

"Welcome, all." said Mr Yen The man liked being dramatic and raised his hands in the air. There were motion sensors in the walls which dimmed the lights. The false walls slid as apart to reveal a forty-eight inch plasma TV. His company logo, a red plus sign, enclosed within a green wreath on a yellow background. After watching this, Martha turned to Alan and said, "Alan I mean no offence, but his presentation is much better than yours." Alan was an experienced businessman and knew how to handle a situation where his competition was being appreciated without getting irritated. He said, "None taken."

Mr Yen began, "Today, my friends, were here to discuss the motives of the expedition and to get the consent of the crew." The occupants of the room nodded.

The man continued after straightening his tie, "Firstly the main reason for this expedition is to unravel the secrets of the Chorés islands. As in the Bermuda triangle expedition, where we found certain sea creatures which had never been catalogued before, we plan to find new species of flora and fauna here too." There was a slight pause as a few heads turned towards Delton and Martha. Once he was sure that he had their attention, Mr Yen said. "We also hope to find plants, in particular, ones that can cure diseases and bring us some profits. Secondly we think that getting a better understanding of the phenomenon there could help us understand the universe and our own planet much better." Andrew smiled. This man had put it well, but Andrew's first priority would be to find that dragon. For a second he wondered what the others would say when they heard him and Alan tell them about the dragon that very moment. The thought made him smile.

Mr Yen was now walking towards the screen. He used a complicated set of hand gestures which the motion sensors picked up and allowed him to manipulate the display of the screen. Now it showed a document next to the faces of each of the crew members except Alan. Mr Yen explained, "Our brave crew members have to sign their consent and also agree that the investors are not responsible for their lives." This made a few of them swallow. The possible death waiting for them was always a grim subject to talk about. "If you wish not to risk your lives, now is the time to call out."

That made Alan remember what his namesake had said back in Portland.

This made everyone think for a while. Martha who was generally quiet was first to speak, "Mr Yen, I have dedicated three years of my life to the study of plants and animals to improve our situation and theirs. I need just a little more data which I have not found anywhere in the world. I simply cannot miss this opportunity. My life is my responsibility. I shall sign my consent."

Andrew spoke next, "I have always been one to step up to discovery. There is something in the islands. Something to be found. I shall sign too." This made Andrew seem like an adrenaline loving adventurer. Only Alan understood the hidden meaning.

Patrick was next, "Knowledge, according to me is power. I wish to give this power to the world. To uncover the truth and impart it. I shall sign too." What Patrick may have left out was that his motivation included beating Delton.

Delton's motive was simple, "I want to learn what lies there. As humans we must forge ahead and discover. I merely want to be a part of it." These words were genuine and a few of them clapped. Stealing the attention once again.

Alex Maple in general was a self-satisfied, confident individual. In brief, the exact opposite of his brother. He stood up and placed his palms on the table and leaned forward before saying, "One thing that history has thought us is that for major discoveries to be made, we need equipment. It's just that my equipment is the best and none of you would be able to operate it as well as me." Alan elbowed Alex which made him wince. He then added, "I also want the fame, okay? There I said it. I'll sign." Though this sounded slightly impolite, it was Alex's way of saying that he really wanted to go just for the fun of it.

The investors believed them. Mr Yen clapped once and two men came running in with a briefcase. Mr Yen typed in a combination and the case opened, revealing some documents. One of the men took them out and gave it to the expedition members. He also handed each of them a pen and then the two newcomers left the room with another clap from Mr Yen.

The five crew members prayed for a second and signed. This moment sealed their fate. Even the Harandels can't predict the future of a particular universe until a certain point in time. This was such a point. You may be wondering what Harandels are, but all in good time.

The lights came on as soon as they signed and the wall closed again. "This is it, huh Alan?" asked Alex. Mr Sawner was too overwhelmed to reply. Now that they had signed, the gravity of the situation struck him. He realized that in a way their lives rested in his hands. Though the document stated that he and his investors were not responsible, his consciousness would kill him. Should he tell them about the dragon and let them decide? No it was too late for that now.

The investors and crew members all were now heading to the press meet. The elevator descended down its shaft, directly to the parking lot. The group boarded four cars and the convoy drove off towards the Tai O public pier.

The beach gleamed along to the left on Shek Tsai Po street on the way to the pier. They were just a few minutes from their destination. It was nearly 9'o clock. They passed a fish market on the way and a tuna smashed onto the windshield of the first car. Alex, who was siding in passenger seat next to the driver yelped in a humiliating manner and said, "What the fish?" This would have been almost humorous if not for the number of fishes being thrown at the car by onlookers from the market. The cars managed to drive away safely.

Alan asked the driver, "What was that all about?" the driver tilted his head and replied, "They are a local group of hippies sir. They believe that your expedition will bring death and that's just their way of protesting." Again, people warning them. Well, Alan could bear his own death in this expedition but he couldn't begin to imagine causing the death of the others.

They reached the pier which was filled by more people than they had ever anticipated. The press meet was to be held in a large tent.

As they stepped out of the car Delton turned his head to the sea. There it was…in the distance, the Tenebris Chorés islands. Six smaller ones surrounding the large central island, their destination that would be the centre of the world's attention. The crowd screamed at the sight of the crew members stepping onto the pier.

Alan, being used to the attention raised his hand. They were escorted by security guards into the tent. There was a large wooden stage with twelve seats. Montres walked over to Alan and said, "We trust you my friend." Victor, Rahul, Lai Chee and Montres all walked in. They were followed by the crew. The journalists, cameramen and photographers were already present. The people took their respective seats. Alan walked up to the dais. One of his employees handed him his papers. Under all the pressure, Alan felt a moment of joy. He was making history. On the first row he saw his mother, she had the same eyes as him, but blonde hair. He also distinguished the families of the others. He wished this moment would last forever and they wouldn't have to go. Alas time doesn't wait for anyone. Actually it would if…I'll save it for later.

Alan began the speech by saying, "Good morning ladies and gentlemen. Today we are all here to mark this historic day. I am proud to be part of this expedition dedicated to the solve the mystery of the Tenebris Chorés islands." Then he thanked his investors and their respective companies. Then he gave a short note on the crew's bravery. His exact words are missing in the records that I received. Thus I leave it to your imagination.

After the initial speech, the questions began. The journalists raised their hands and Alan picked a man in a dark blue suit and a grey tie. He said, "Sir, any comment for those who are calling you an attention seeker?" Alan had prepared for this one, "Well, I would say that they are seriously mistaken. An attention seeker, by me, is one who is never satisfied with the attention he receives. I merely wish to go to the island to explore and not to get the world to know me, they already do. If I recall correctly, one of my employees leaked the matter on the internet long before I had intended too. In fact I had only wished to let the world know after the expedition was over." Journalists wrote down every word and the video cameras broadcasted his reply live, throughout the world.

The next question was regarding the island, "What do you hope to find out there?" Alan had prepared for this one too, "The island, for now, is a mystery. If you had meant 'what we are trying to find', then the answer would be different types of plants and animals that might be useful to us in developing medicines. Also discovering the cause of the disappearances." This was pretty much what they had talked about in the private conference but it was enough for the journalists.

There were several other questions. Alan too, patiently answered each of them. He was almost glad for the continuous volley of questions heading his way. It helped divert his mind.

Finally it was time for the kids session of the meet. Alan relaxed a bit. Kids always came up with creative questions which were tough to predict. The journalists on the other hand tensed up, waiting like preying vultures to see if one of the children could give Alan a tough time with his/her question.

Alan then thanked each and every school in turn for their funds that made the expedition possible.

This was it. The time had come. William kept saying to himself, "Don't flop it." He just prayed not to stammer or make grammatical errors while posing his question. He simply couldn't afford to embarrass himself in front of the world. He put his pen in his school blazer. He was just two turns away now.

Alan was halfway through the student session. Some kids had come up with some crazy questions which are better left out.

A boy asked, "Mr Sawner, my name is Shiazo Ping. I wanted to ask you if it will be possible for you to keep radio contact after you get onto the island?" Alex had assured him that they would, but he decided to stay on the safe side, "We are using a type of communication device that hasn't been implemented there before, but it should most probably be functional within the usual blackout zone."

Next a boy with dark hair and brown eyes stood up. His skin was slightly tanned as though he had been playing at the beach for a whole day. He said, "Good afternoon Mr Sawner, my name is William Silver. My question to you is that, are you going to catalogue your journey and later make it available to the public after the expedition comes to an end?" Alan was thrilled. He had been silently praying for someone to pop up with the question. He said, "An excellent question William. Even till yesterday, I have been recording the events of my journey in great detail and shall publish it as a book once this whole affair comes to an end." The audience clapped and the boy took his seat. For some reason this kid reminded Alan of himself. "Next question." he said and the session continued for another hour.

By 2'o clock the meet had come to an end. Alan and the rest of the crew headed to a separate tent for lunch. The spectators went to a nearby restaurant to eat.

They were scheduled to leave at fifteen past three. Their camper had been shipped to the fourth outer island. They would be taking a boat till there, then a boat with the camper on it to the main island.

The crew had opted for a seven course meal. There was a good chance that it might as well be their last, why not enjoy it?

As he walked in with the others, Alan saw the boy, William walking towards the restaurant with his assigned teacher. He wanted to tell him something and jogged over to catch up. He requested the teacher to allow him to talk to Willaim. He called him aside and said, "William, do you remember what I said about publishing a book about the expedition once it was over?" The boy nodded. "You remind me a lot of myself and I promise to send you the first copy." William was thrilled. The nine year old's reply was something like this, "Thank you Mr Sawner. I can't tell you how much this means to me." "Its okay. Take care now." with this last sentence he went back to join his friends.

They ate, talked and laughed, for a brief half-an-hour they forgot their burdens and sorrows and felt like proper friends. After lunch they each went a different way to meet their families.

Alan's mother was wearing a white dress and a hat. A necklace of pearls adorned her neck. "Alan my boy," she said and ran towards him, embracing her son. "how are you? I've missed you." She took a step back and wiped a tear off Alan's cheek which he hadn't even been aware of. "I'm doing just fine mum. What do you think?" said Alan. "Your little trip is rather impressive, but promise me you'll be fine." Alan hated promising things that he wasn't sure of, especially to his mother but he said, "I promise mum." They talked for a while, about other things. Like Alan's childhood and happy times with his father. Their encounter may seem a bit dramatic, but the circumstances were so and his mother couldn't help getting a little emotional.

Andrew and the rest of them had similar visits. A few tears were shed with warm words and promises that may or may not be fulfilled. Finally it was 3'o clock and the time had come for them to leave.

The pier was twice as crowded as before and there were people along the length of the entire beach. The atmosphere was electric. There was a raised platform in the centre. They climbed on and Alan spoke just two sentences into the microphone, "Its time for us to leave. Wish the expedition success." As a response there were several cheers and claps. Alan would definitely have enjoyed some background music as they walked down the platform. Then they could have pretended that this whole thing was just a movie and possible death wasn't waiting for them.

They boarded a modified yacht. It was fairly large and could have housed many people, but currently its only passengers were the captain, a few guards, the crew and Alan's investors. The investors were to accompany them only to the outer island and no further.

It was going to take a while. The crew walked up to the top deck, leaving the investors downstairs. The sun shone brightly. Martha walked up to the rail and placed her elbows on it. Everyone had changed to camouflage outfits and looked quite like soldiers. She said, "I was tensed all the way till now, but now that we're here and the whole thing is inevitable, I'm barely nervous." The others could relate to it. They felt the same way. A while later the captain announced that they were going to arrive in a few minutes and requested the passengers to prepare themselves to disembark.

The small island was a flurry of activity. The ground buzzed with various squadrons preparing their transport to the main island. Alex ran ahead to help the *knuckleheads* as he called them. He had designed most of the equipment and was afraid that they might break it. Patrick was delighted to know that they had arrived on the side of the island where his seismic sensor was.

He ran over inspect some data. The group followed. Patrick told them that there was a change in the configuration to be made. He said, "The wonderful thing about these is that they have a slot where I can update the software. I'd asked Marcus to send me the memory stick just in case we came by this one." The memory stick had been in the package that he had received but it wasn't the only thing there.

They had later been escorted to the second boat. It had a flat side on which the silver camper stood. The boat would reach the island during high tide. They would anchor it down and once the tide receded, they would drive onto the island and the exploration could begin.

Alex climbed into the control room and typed in a few commands to the on board computers and pushed the throttle. Their luggage and equipment had already been loaded onto the camper. The boat set off towards their final destination.

The sunset was beautiful, but they weren't there for the scenery. They were there on a mission.

Chapter 8

JOLLY ROGER

It was nearly sunset when the tide drew back far enough for the Tenebris Chorés island expedition members to set foot on the island itself. Alan Sawner was the first. He hadn't vanished or gone mad…so far so good. All these months of speculations and it felt like any other beach in the world. The fewest disappearances had occurred on that face of the island, so their odds were better there. Andrew Briston and Delton Kraig got down next. Martha Frost entered the camper, their specially modified exploration vehicle. The Maple brothers lowered the ramp for the camper to drive onto the island.

Once Martha had driven the camper off the boat, the rest of the crew got in. Alex checked the status of their communication devices and said, "The communication devices are operational and we are good to go." Alan had somewhat become the commanding authority. No one had decided this, it was just that the expedition was Alan's idea and he was their employer apart from being their friend. He was a capable businessman and his ability to make the right decisions under pressure made him the ideal leader.

Alan got to a spot where everyone could see him, "Well people, we're here. Now we have to get organised to make sure that this turns out successful. Tonight we're just going to enter the cliff wall. This wall formed by the steep cliffs of the island has only two entrances, this one and one that is on the other side of the island which will be our exit. Tomorrow we will be driving further in. Delton and Patrick will be setting up their equipment to study the phenomenon and Alex, you are supposed to help them. Andrew will accompany Martha into the jungle to collect samples for study. Does anyone have any suggestions to add?" Alex spoke first, "I think its a good plan. We get to do the most work in the shortest time." Andrew and Patrick said in unison, "I agree." Delton and Martha also stated their consent in the plan. "So for now, we have to drive till we reach the other side of the cliff wall, right?" Andrew asked. Alan replied with a single word, "Yes."

Andrew drove as he had experience navigating through jungles. As they progressed, Martha told him to stop.

Dr Frost had seen a plant which looked familiar to a type that she had once seen as a fossil in a book. She had first thought that she was mistaken, but she saw it again. A tree that had gone extinct millions of years ago was standing tall and strong. She reached into one of the draws which contained their equipment and took out the syringe like tool she had shown Alan and the others at her greenhouse in Paris. She opened the door and reached out to a low hanging branch. She pressed a small button and a tiny needle injected itself into the branch. It scanned the cells and displayed the scientific name of the tree. Below it a text in red said, 'status: extinct'. This startled Martha and she almost jumped in excitement. She cried, "Everyone, come here, quick!" They others rushed over to see what it was. She explained it to an astonished group of men. They were barely an hour into the expedition and already had proof that there was something special about the plants of the island.

Martha got out of the camper to get a closer look. Then out of nowhere, a light shone from in front of the camper. "What's that?" asked Delton. "It looks like a flashlight, but it can't be people, can it?" said Andrew. Alex took a step towards the windshield and said, "Should we go check?" Alan replied, "What do you think?" This question was directed at Patrick. He didn't want to look like a coward and said, "Lets go." Alan was slightly more cautious and said, "Someone should stay here just in case...just in case something happens." "I'll stay. I'm examining the plants anyway." said Martha. They agreed and the men pushed through the branches and leaves towards the source of the light.

Alan was at the head of the group. As he pushed the last of the leaves apart, he saw a sight that made him doubt his eyes. The others stood in a semicircle around him.

There were several cars and huge shipping crates filled with what looked like guns. There were also several men holding rifles and handguns. There was a small warehouse-like structure located a few hundred yards away. It was brightly lit. There was a large metal wall that extended as far as they could see. "Who are they?" asked Alex. "I don't know but I'm sure that this little set up of theirs is illegal." "Pirates," said Andrew, "they're criminals who used to work alone. Thieves and murderers without a gang got together to form one. I heard rumours that they had their base on some island near Hong Kong. I had absolutely no clue though that they were here."

The question now was how they were going to avoid them. Alan came up with an answer, "Lets drive along the inside of the cliff wall and see if there is an opening within this metal one of theirs." They all agreed.

The five men walked carefully to the left, treading around branches and leaves. They froze as they heard a man rasp behind them, "Stop! Don't move. Now slowly turn around." They followed the instructions. Patrick was closest to the man and felt it wise to attempt a rescue. He turned around and performed a clumsy punch directed at the man's solar plexus. It wasn't the best of shots but it was enough to put him out for the time being. "We need to get out of here now." said Delton and they turned around to be greeting by half a dozen men with pistols. They opened fire, The crew members had nowhere to hide and they fell to the ground like stones.

71

In reality the criminals hadn't fired bullets but tranquilliser darts. Then the intruders had been carried away to the main quarters which was the warehouse like building they had seen earlier. The men had been tied up and were to be left under guard till they woke up again.

Alex had been the first to come back around. His eyelids were heavy and his shoulder throbbed. He saw Alan and the others. Alex nudged Andrew with his good shoulder and woke him up too. Their mouths weren't taped so they could at least speak. Calling for help would be stupid though. The criminals and they were the only ones on the island. Even if they didn't return, they would be mistaken for one of the usual disappearances. They had to get out.

Alan was the last to snap out of it. He looked at the other four men. Martha wasn't there, so he assumed that she was still free and their only possible hope of rescue.

Their ears rung with the sound of their guard banging the barrel of his gun against the bars of the cell. He yelled something in Chinese which they failed to understand. It would translate to: *On your feet. The boss is coming. Get up.* His supposed boss turned up at the entrance. A man in a black suit wearing sunglasses and a costly watch. He ram a hand across his bald head and spoke in English, "Who are you?" Patrick was the first to reply, "Don't you watch TV?" The man found that question amusing and said, "No, I'm afraid we're somewhat disconnected from the rest of the world."

Alan saw an opportunity there. They weren't aware of their identities. This could be used to their advantage. There was always the possibility that the man was trying to mislead them but it was worth a try. Before anyone could say anything, Alan looked at the man and began, "We're thieves. We heard rumours about a group...your group being here on this island. We came here too see if it was real and if so, join said group."

The story had been somewhat convincing but the man needed more, "I see, but that still doesn't explain why you attacked my man." Alan strained himself to come up with an answer, quick.

He said, "We weren't sure who he was. Since he was holding a gun at us, we had to assume was an enemy. Please understand." The man thought for a while and his face now wore an expression that Alan knew all too well. He had bought it.

They were later released and were taken to a large dining hall. They sat with the boss and found themselves surprisingly hungry. After gobbling up a few cheeseburgers and pizzas, the lot of them leaned back in their chairs for a chat.

The crew members introduced themselves using a combination original first names and fake last names. They even went through a sort of oath taking ceremony that officially added them to the gang's ranks. They even got guns.

It had turned out that they had been out for an entire night. They were eager to know what Martha had done and if she was OK. A stroke of luck finally came and the boss told them to get familiar with some of the other gang members. They would try to extract some valuable information that might lead to their tickets out of there.

Each of the five men went to different people and introduced themselves using their fake names. The gang had decided to use the island as a base due its existing reputation of disappearances. Soon enough they had discovered that the stories were true. People and other things went missing only after a certain point. They believed that it might be the work of some mysterious animals and that's why the wall had been built. Also it was a stronghold in case any rival gang got word of their existence and decided to attack. They had agents to deliver their food and weapons making them well provisioned and powerful.

The information circulated in Alan's mind and ways of escaping were becoming clearer.

The boss came over to them a while after breakfast and said, "Our agents would have dropped off our food supply in a crate in the forest within a mile from here. You must have heard stories about this place, so I think it will be a good way for you to prove your loyalty by retrieving the food." They had no choice but to obey and they set off.

On the way, the group noticed missiles and various other heavy artillery. Maybe there wasn't anything special about the island. Perhaps these people had shot down planes and sunk ships to create a good cover for themselves. There was no reason why they had to be telling the truth. Though there were many other reasons to oppose this theory, it couldn't be ruled out completely. Alan maintained that there could still be something else to the island, because this theory couldn't explain the change in seismic activity during that flare and the supposedly extinct plant life. Though his main reason to say so, was the Dragon incident which no theory could explain clearly.

They headed down a slope past a vast field if wild grass towards the forest. The recognised the spot where they had been tranquillised, by putting the steel wall to their front and the warehouse to the right. They forged ahead and soon enough, found the camper. They went in to see Martha trying hard to find a signal using the communication device. She looked at them and exclaimed with joy, "You're alive! When I came looking, I saw the men with the guards dragging you to that building. I tried to contact someone but couldn't get a decent signal all night long. How did you escape?" She listened to this with great interest as they told her what had happened.

Martha took a while to grasp this and asked them, "Can't we just go around to the other opening in the wall?" Alan replied to this one, "No. I heard from one the guards that they have the beach and the other opening blocked. The only way is through the gate in the steel blockade that they have under control too. But, they have no radios and have to walk all the way to the other opening, around the cliff wall to communicate. So, if we break through here, drive all the way to the other side through the forest, we can pretend to be new recruits and get off the island."

This plan was next to impossible to execute. They once even considered turning back. Their boat was probably where they had left it, but Andrew told them that the pirates had seized their boat from their outposts on the beach. Now it was on the other opening. This gave them an idea. If they did what Alan had said earlier, they could pretend to have orders from the boss to return to mainland and carry out a secret mission or something, allowing them to escape in their boat.

Alan had more to add. He said, "Do you know why they built that wall?" When no one replied, he continued, "The earlier members of this gang claim that there was something in the forest beyond that supposedly took people away and caused the disappearances of the planes and ships. They built the wall to protect themselves which means that if we get through, they won't follow us. I think we should head into the forest. Even if we don't find anything, at least we'll be able to get through to the other side and escape. I have a plan to get into the forest, past that wall, but it can't be done without your cooperation."

Alan told them what to do. It was risky but it was the best plan they had for success.

The men left Martha in the camper as per plan and headed further into the jungle until they found the crate and hauled it back to the criminal base. The boss was happy and allowed them to have the rest of the day off. Their guard duty started in the evening, so till then they could relax.

They roamed around for a while. Then they put the plan into action and went directly to the gate at lunch time. They knew that their hoax would be discovered soon enough and timing was essential. Alan walked over to one of the guards and said, "The boss wants us to take the shift. Ya'll are dismissed." The guards knew better than to disobey one of the boss's commands even if it came from a newcomer.

Alex had smuggled one of his long range transmitters and signalled for Martha to bring the camper. He used Morse code to transmit the message.

Though this was real life and the odds of the plan going wrong were so infinitesimal, it happened like in one of those fiction novels. The guards weren't accustomed to a sudden change in routine and decided to check with the boss's second in command. The bulky ex-assassin had decided to consult with the boss and the intricately woven threads of the plan began to come apart.

Alan's first view of scene that was rapidly unfolding was of the camper bursting through the trees. Joy flooded through him, but the feeling was immediately suppressed by the dozens of charging men with guns blazing and mortars firing. The scene instantly turned from a peaceful meadow into a battle field. Martha struggled to navigate the camper through the heavy fire.

Alan seemed too dazed to even speak, so Andrew took charge and screamed, "Open the gate." The gate was large enough to allow a truck through to the forest behind and the camper would easily fit through.

In the end it all just came down to a race between the camper and the men. Whichever reached the Alan, Andrew, Delton and the Maples first would decide their fate. To look on the bright side, at least they wouldn't have to act like thieves anymore.

In fact a nasty surprise was waiting store for them. Alan and the others hadn't been there long enough to know that the walls weren't just walls but living quarters. Twenty five of the best members of the gang had the wall quarters. They could be deployed to guard the wall at anytime. This had been in case a rival gang ever knew of the place and decided to attack. These were just five men who couldn't possibly last more than a minute.

A small door opened into the wall and twenty five men jogged out. At last Alan had a stroke of luck. The men were unarmed, but the others and he still had their pistols.

None of the expedition members meant to kill and followed Andrew's lead by shooting at the men's legs. The group had forty bullets among them, eight in each gun. The camper was just a hundred metres away now. They had all run out of ammunition, except Patrick. Their time was running out.

Miraculously they had managed to hold the men back till Martha reached. They opened the door and dived in. The boss and the lower rank members were hopelessly far to do anything. One of the twenty-five muscle men, who wasn't as stupid as the others, pressed the close button for the metal gate. "Drive!" Alan yelled and Martha floored the accelerator. This was going to be close.

Hydraulic pumps pushed the massive steel slabs closer every second. If a truck tried to squeeze through now, it wouldn't be able to. The camper entered the tiny square of space. Sparks flew as the closing doors scraped the paint off the sides.

Alan had closed his eyes, but when he opened them, there was forest to their sides and ahead of them. The base behind the wall was far away now and Alan hoped for some good luck.

Patrick had gotten up and was walking towards Alan now. This drew the attention of the others and they absently stared. Alan turned to him. Patrick spoke, "Alan, you do realize that we might have died, right?" Alan was a bit taken aback, but said, "Yeah, it was a close call for all of us, but the important thing is that we made it out alive, huh?"

It was only when Patrick turned around that they saw his expression. He was furious and this time he screamed, "We could have died and its all your fault. You got us into signing that agreement and trailing after you here. I expected a nice field where I could set down my seismic recorders and have some coffee as I worked out some equations on my laptop. Not fighting criminals and near death."

Martha stopped the camper and the other got up. Patrick drew his gun and brought it in line with Alan's head.

This situation had just morphed from bad to worse in a matter of seconds.

Chapter 9

IS THAT IT?

One's day can be called officially ruined when a gun is pointed at your face. The pirates that had set up base on the Tenebris Chorés central island had captured Alan and his crew.

Alan's expedition had been directed to find the cause of the countless disappearances on the island and had run into the pirates.

On the occasion of the crew's escape, the pirates had nearly killed them. Patrick Maple blamed Alan for dragging them into that mess and was now pointing a gun at his forehead. Alan's day was officially ruined.

This new development forced the other crew members into action. Alan was too stunned to speak, let alone defend himself. Andrew reacted first. He elbowed Patrick in the side of his gut. The geologist crashed to the floor but was still conscious. With one hand, he clutched the point where Andrew's elbow had struck and with the other, he tried to reach for the gun. He eventually managed to say, "Don't you see? He's trying to get us killed." Andrew wasn't going to let Patrick make false accusations against his friend, "How? How did you speculate that he's trying to get us killed. Even if he wanted to, why?" Patrick's mind knew that

Andrew was right, but something told him that Alan was the enemy. "I don't know." He spat that last sentence out as he raised the gun once again, shifting it between Alan and Andrew, trying to decide who his enemy was. He soon came to the conclusion that it was Alan and took aim. Then as though by a miracle, he fell to the floor.

Martha Frost had stabbed Patrick with a syringe containing a tranquilliser. "He'll be out for a few hours." she had said. A while later, Alex had found a dart on his brother's leg. Martha, being a biologist took it to the analysing equipment and began working on deciphering its composition.

Delton was feeling a bit useless lately. They had parked in a small clearing, waiting for Patrick to get up again. The dart had contained a drug which was the cause for Patrick's stunt with the gun earlier. The expedition crew couldn't help, but wonder if they had gotten out of the frying pan and into the fire by venturing further towards the heart of the jungle.

Delton had decided to set up his equipment and see if he could do something productive. Martha was still busy, trying to see if the dart may contain anything life threatening or may have any side effects. Alan and Andrew were discussing something in hushed tones. Alex Maple was sitting on his workbench in the camper, working on building some tiny device.

It was around 3'o clock when Patrick regained consciousness. The crew took a lunch break. They set up a table outside the camper and sat down. Alex told his brother what had happened. Patrick was a bit ashamed if what he had done. When Delton had tried to console him, he had snapped back. Perhaps the drug hadn't worn out completely.

After a good meal, Delton stood up to get everyone's attention and said, "Alan, I heard you tell Andrew that you knew about the men in the wall all along. If that's true, why didn't you tell us?"

Each member of their little crew responded differently to this latest statement. Martha had said, "Is it true Alan?" Patrick's reply was, "Stop joking around Dr Kraig." Alex just stared.

Alan looked at Andrew and he nodded encouragingly. The message was clear, *Tell them.* "Yes it is true. I knew." Delton leaned forward and banged the table with a fist, "Then why didn't you just tell us? We could have just gone back and tried to get a signal to contact the government to get some soldiers over." This was a lot to take in and for the first time ever, Patrick agreed with him and said, "We have food enough for weeks. Its not like we can't do that now."

Alan was beginning to worry that the crew might get too angry on him. There was no choice but to tell them the truth now. He began, "Alright everyone, I'm about to tell you something. This at sound impossible to believe but I swear its true. The other opening of the wall isn't blocked and our boat was right there. We could have turned back right there."

Before Alan could get to the part about the dragon, Delton interrupted, "So you're saying that the other opening was free for us to enter and we could have simply circled around and went into the island, continuing with the expedition or could have just left?" Alan said in a slightly less than lively tone, "Please, let me complete. Did you hear about the tsunami in Jakarta?" "Yes." they replied as a chorus.

The next half-an-hour passed as Alan described the incident in great detail and how the dragon had told them to use only one of the openings and leave only through the other. Also of how it had warned them not to enter through one then leave and enter through the other, unless they wished to die.

Delton and Alex believed him to some extent, though Martha and for Patrick were a bit sceptical. Delton then said, "I believe this. Mind you, I'm not saying that what happened to you in Jakarta or the disappearances here are supernatural, but I for one have always believed that the sheer size and number of planets of the universe may have allowed sentient life to evolve and that dragon may be such a creature." Patrick couldn't resist a smile, "Are you suggesting that its an alien?" "Yes." said Delton. Alex nodded, "That does explain why the pirates feared some mysterious creature here. My only concern is whether we must be afraid as well." Martha decided to remain neutral and said, "I am inclined to agree with Delton. After all I found supposedly extinct plants, but your story has a few missing blanks Alan. Such as, what might be wrong with walking out of the entrance and going back in the other way?" Andrew being the only other witness spoke about the matter for the first time, "He said we would find the answers to all our questions when we find him." Patrick chuckled and said, "Well I guess the pirates must have hit you with a hallucination dart too. That explains the case of that boy, Christopher Marques.

The missing planes and ships could have just been the work of the Pirates They have some serious weaponry. Though he told you that it was some mysterious creature, do you think anyone tells a newbie everything? It could have just been a popular legend."

Patrick's argument was pretty valid. Martha sided with him for the time being. It was going to be so only till they met the beast, but for now let's stick to the present. Miss Frost said, "I agree with Patrick. So is that it? Is there nothing special about this place, except an expertly hidden pirate base?" "What about the change in seismic activity and that flare?" suggested Delton. Patrick had a reply coming up, "If those guys smuggled missiles onto this place without the government noticing, I'm pretty sure they could have got the equipment to fake that flare and cheat the recording devices. If you remember they're located on the outer islands where people are allowed." "No one could have cheated my equipment." protested Alex. Martha turned towards him now and took on the expression of a sympathetic big sister and said, "Now Alex, there are always new people coming into the field. It's not a universal law that no one can hack into your gadgets."

Alan and Andrew stood idle as the other members took it upon themselves to continue the debate. Alan decided to step in before this turned into a fight, "Listen. We can argue about this later. The only way out anyway if through the other opening, so let's forge ahead. We can look for signs to see if there may be any other causes on the way and we can solve this conflict later."

The group had wasted an hour arguing about this and knew that Alan was right. They went back into the camper and each took a seat. Andrew drove and their journey progressed.

They could have escaped, but Alan and Andrew had lied because of some imaginary dragon. This is what the others thought. Actually Alan and Andrew had done it in order to make sure that everyone followed what the dragon had instructed them to do. Find it within the island, without leaving through the same entrance of the cliff wall as the one through which they entered. If they broke these rules, the world would be destroyed This was almost comical. How would the entrance make a difference? The others wouldn't have agreed if they had told the truth. They would think the two of them to be mad.

Since the other end wasn't blocked, they had all the time in the world. Why not try to solve the mystery of the island? After all that's what they were there for.

That evening Martha decided to head out into the forest to see if she could find any nocturnal animals. Andrew went with her to help. She was using sound waves to search for any new animals that might use echolocation. Again it was the only one in existence and built by Alex.

Patrick was busy, trying to get some seismic readings and collected samples of the earth up to ten feet underground.

Both of them weren't too convinced with Alan's fairytale, but nor did they completely believe that the pirates were the sole reason for the disappearances. They wanted to find the truth.

Alex and Delton were working together at operating a device to measure the gravity of the place and also look for any higher than usual traces of isotopes.

Alan was sitting on the roof of the camper, looking at the crew working hard to get results, feeling lonely, bored and pretty stupid.

A while later, the crew heard a loud shriek. It sounded like Martha. They abandoned their tasks and ran to the source of the voice.

The four of them broke through the last of the vines and were greeted by a magnificent sight. There were huge, seemingly bioluminescent animals. They were about the size of elephants, probably a little larger. They had a similar body structure too. They had four legs. The hind legs seemed a bit different. They also had two triple jointed, arm like structures protruding from the joints of their fore legs. They had thick fur which also seemed to glow. Their heads resembled a tiger's or any other big cat's. Curved horns extended from the heads. There was something different about them though. Their eyes were missing.

The flabbergasted group stared, transfixed by the animals' beauty. Alan noticed Martha and Andrew standing in a ditch a few yards away. He climbed down into it, making sure to have a good footing. The creatures had hooves which he hadn't noticed before. What were these things?

"Martha, Andrew." he called out to them. They had pretty stunned expressions as well. The moon was visible too now. Its light revealed a river which now gleamed like a silver snake. Martha signed for him to be quiet by placing a finger to her lips.

Alan didn't realize why but he tried to be as silent as possible. He walked closer and asked, "What are these things?" Andrew whispered back, "We don't know, but they're definitely not what they appear. Do you see that?" He pointed at a patch of flesh, bones and blood. The sight would have given any five year old nightmares for days. Alan silently promised to do his best to stay away from whatever did that. He couldn't resist asking, "What did that?" Andrew's finger turned towards one of the glowing elephant/goat/tiger and said, "That." It almost seemed out of a movie that something which looked so peaceful could cause the death of another animal. Then again most animals in nature were so. Another perfect example for the saying, 'Never judge a book by its cover.'.

"Hey, are you seeing this?" screamed Alex. A bunch of 'hsst's sounded from Andrew and Martha. It took a second for Alan to realize that the creatures may not have eyes, but had ears and most definitely hear them.

The single scream had been enough to attract the attention of the creatures. The turned towards them and let of a high pitched screeches like the one you might expect from bats. It had turned out that they used echolocation and that's how Martha and Andrew had located them.

The day was getting weirder and weirder for the group. Alex, his brother and Delton were on the edge of the ditch when the animals had turned and charged. They had gone from tame to terrifying in moments. First, they stopped glowing, but the moon was bright enough to allow them to see the beasts sprout long tusks and the extra limbs sprouted claws. It turned out that the creatures were bipeds and had been crouching. They stood up to their full height and had an uncanny resemblance to dinosaurs without tails.

The turned towards the men and charged at them. To the creatures, they were intruders that had infiltrated their territory. Or food. Possibly both. The group had no choice but to turn and run.

The creatures were persistent and weren't going to rest until the threat had been eliminated. There had been about six of them when they had been in the clearing by that river. Two of the same creatures had now appeared from nowhere and blocked their path to the camper. The crew had their backs to each other and were being herded together. Classic behaviour of predators that hunt in packs. Now one of them, probably the leader was going to go in for the kill. The others would prevent the prey from escaping.

After all the trouble they had been through, it had come down to this, death by glowing half dino- half elephant.

Alan closed his eyes and expected death. He then experienced a similar feeling as before the tsunami had crashed down on them back in Jakarta. The moon seemed to dim by a bit and out of the shadows, a large purple, scaled arm with talons pierced the gut of one of the beasts and it crashed to the ground.

The animals decided that this new attacker was more dangerous than the pathetic little humans.

The shadows seemed to rise and take the shape of a purple dragon which bore a striking resemblance to the description that

Alan had given of the dragon he had seen after the tsunami in Jakarta, except the colour was wrong.

The creature had black eyes that seemed to see right through their souls and claim them for itself.

The monstrous dragon was fierce and ripped the creatures to shreds. One of the monsters managed to land a blow with it's horns. The dragon turned and hefted it with all four limbs. The shadows seemed to take the shape of a serpentine tail which had a menacing, spear-like, razor sharp end. It pierced right through the poor animal and the last of them was no more.

The crew had been terrified of what they had seen of the glowing beasts, but there no word to describe the absolute terror that this creature instilled in them. It had dispensed of eight of the other animals with such efficiency that it scared them. They wondered how long it might take for it to kill them if mistook them for enemies.

The purple dragon did turn to them and it spoke. This was nothing like the gentle, soothing voice that the red dragon had possessed. This was cold and heartless. This life sucking voice said, "Greetings humans. The Crenobels attacking you were rather unexpected and could not be allowed to kill you just yet." The crew had to take it that the Crenobels were the glow elephants that had until recently, been set on killing them. So did that mean this dragon was their ally?

This time it addressed Alan and Andrew. The others were pushed back a few metres by some invisible force that was seemingly under the dragon's control as it moved its hand in sync with the it. It said, "You humans realize that when my brother spoke to you, he was referring only to the two of you. You were supposed to come here to look for him alone. There would have been no confusion at all. Not with them. Now their lives cannot be guaranteed. It is up to him to decide whether to let all of you through or not. It is imperative that you reach the entrance. They may come along, but may not be worthy enough to travel beyond it. You have two days from now. None can leave this island now. It is sealed."

The information was a little complicated to comprehend. So according to the dragon, Alan and Andrew were meant to find its *brother* (possibly the red dragon) alone and should not have brought the other crew members as their lives couldn't be guaranteed. The *entrance* probably lead to the place where they could find his brother. Even if the others went along, may not be let through and there were only two days to get there and who was *he,* the one who would decide whether to let them in or not. Two of them were guaranteed to live (probably Alan and Andrew), but what of the others?

There were quite a few questions to be asked, but before anyone could ask them the dragon continued, "I have just one more thing to tell you. Make sure to have a keen eye as you head on. You will need to get the key from him to enter. You must insert the key into the entrance by sunset in two more days. The entrance itself shall open when the time is right. He is your only hope. When the time comes, you must either be inside the entrance or shall perish with the rest of this island. I shall meet you at the entrance once it is opened."

"He?" Andrew asked. The dragon turned towards him and replied, "Yes. He is called the watcher."

Now this dragon was asking them to look for that person and get a key to let them through the entrance or they would die? Who gave it the rights to order them around? Then it leaned closer to Alan and Andrew and said something which only one of the others heard, "Only two of the six have been tested and have proven themselves worthy, though I can't say who. The lives of the others depends on the watcher's decision. He will guide you.

I must also warn you. The key must be placed into the entrance by sunset on that day. The watcher will tell you when to enter."

Then for a brief second Alan and Andrew thought that they saw something in the dragon's eyes, but it hadn't been there long enough for them to see.

In a fraction of a second, the whole body of the creature seemed to turn into a liquid and fall into the shadows once again.

This left the crew standing in the forest. It took the loud roar of some creature to make them walk back to the camper. The day had been extremely tiresome and strange. Well at least one thing was clear now. Alan had been telling the truth.

They hadn't spoken much over dinner. If the island was going to perish soon and their only hope was to find this so called watcher and get the key to some entrance, they would do it. If a human had said this, they would have taken him for an MRI scan, but its hard to ignore when said by a fifty foot, purple dragon that supposedly hadn't existed until they had seen it.

Alan and Andrew had been affected worse by the incident. Two would be let through, but the others would have to stay back. Alan and Andrew had seen the red dragon first and were the most likely to get through. The entire island was to be destroyed and they would be behind the entrance and be safe, would those left outside have to die? This had struck the other crew members too and they decided to set it aside for the time being and focus on finding this watcher character. If they just sat there, they would die anyway. If at least two of them were going to survive, it was worth the risk. They were genuinely ready to make the sacrifice, except one of them. The dragon had said that two would be allowed through. Why couldn't he be one of the two?

As everyone climbed into their respective bunks, several thoughts went through their minds. Each of them pulled the curtains shut and drifted deep into sleep.

They had decided to look for the watcher the next day. Matters were uncertain at the time, but one thing was for sure... they weren't going down easy.

Chapter 10

THE WATCHER

The morning had been a maelstrom of activity. Alan Sawner was helping Alex wire in some thermal sensors to the roof of the camper. Andrew and the rest had split into two teams and decided to look for the watcher in the forest.

They only had a day left now. The island was supposedly sealed off by the dragon and everything on it would be destroyed in a day. Of course, they checked to see if the entrances in the cliff wall were still there, but they had mysteriously disappeared. The expedition crew's only hope was to find someone called the watcher who held the key to some entrance that would save them.

According to the mysterious dragon, two of them had passed some kind of test and would be allowed to enter but it was up to the watcher to decide the fate of the other members. They had all pretty much come to the conclusion that Alan and Andrew were the two that bad been chosen for salvation. After all they had seen a similar dragon, in Jakarta, when a tsunami had crashed down on them. That one had instructed Alan and Andrew to find it in the island.

Their current status was rather uncertain. They were all still trying to get the previous day's events out of their heads. Now they had a tough job with a fast approaching deadline. One of the group had even had nightmares about the glow elephants.

Patrick and Martha returned first. "Any sign of him?" asked Alan. "No. Not even animals." Out of nowhere, Delton's voice sounded, "It is sealed. Andrew and I trekked to the top of that hill again to check if the openings had reappeared. No sign of an opening anywhere. Even the steel wall is missing. There's only rock all around us. We're in a cage." Martha uselessly suggested another idea which they had already considered, "Can't we try climbing to the top of the cliff and get out?" Andrew who had also seemingly appeared from thin air sighed and said, "Martha, we've considered this before. That cliff is as smooth as polished marble. We can't even attempt it without climbing gear, which we don't have. Even if we did, it would be too risky."

The disappointed crew sat down at the table that they had used for breakfast. Each of them, searching desperately, for a way off the island. They all eventually came to the same conclusion, the watcher had to be found.

It was well after lunch time that the crew, who had decided to look further out, reached the tiny hut. There was a small clearing outside the hut with a broad ring drawn into the ground. They naturally assumed that it belonged to the watcher. It was the only lead that they had and decided to stay there till the watcher returned. All of this was obviously based on the theory that this hut belonged to him.

The bushes at a distance rustled and everyone stood up and turned towards it. The leaves parted to let a boy with dark hair and green eyes, probably no older than fourteen, into the camp. He was wearing a casual, white, silk shirt and blue jeans. "I've been looking for you. You shouldn't have left your vehicle. Do you have any idea how tough it is to locate six people on such a large island." The boy was talking to them like one would to a bunch of old friends.

Andrew spoke first, "Who are you? Are you lost?" The kid chuckled and said, "I expected you to recognise me and no, I am not lost." There was something about the boy that made him seem older than he looked. Alan realized it and immediately said it out loud, "You're the watcher." The boy nodded and said, "Finally. Actually that's a title. My name is Bardos."

The group had expected some creature or at least a tall, fierce looking man to be the watcher. Not some kid.

Alex chose to get things moving and said, "The dragon asked us to get some sort of a key to an entrance. According to him, two of us had passed some kind of trial and you would decide about the rest and let us pass through."

The boy leaped onto a nearby rock and replied, "It's not as simple as that dear Alex. The thing is that you must pass my trial as well to enter. Mainly mine. Now two of you may have passed according to the Harandel, but according to me, none of you have proved yourself worthy. So I have a few tests for you to attend. Those who pass, shall be allowed to enter."

This was just great. Now *none* of their fates were certain. They had to attend a test that was a matter of life and death… literally. Makes you feel a whole lot better about your middle school physics exam. Another bit of interesting information was that the dragon-like creature was called a Harandel. As though that bit of knowledge could be of any use in that situation.

They had no choice in the matter and agreed to take the test. The boy seemed very excited, "Excellent," he had said, "but be warned, it won't be easy. This will test something that I call human clarity." Patrick was getting tired of this chatter and said, "Okay, okay, just get on with it." "Alright. First is a little sparing. The rules are simple, don't step out of the ring. First to make contact wins. What about you?" said Bardos, pointing at Delton. The astrophysicist was uncertain of what to do and so stepped forward. The boy spoke again, "I'll be right back."

Bardos had run into the hut and come out holding an arm's length blade with a handle at both ends. He grabbed each and pulled the weapon into two individual blades. He threw one to Delton who caught it in mid-air expertly.

Delton took a step forward and bent his knees to lower his centre of gravity and increase his balance. Something told him not to underestimate the kid standing before him, swinging the sword with a single hand. As he walked, Bardos said, "Well Delton, your certificate in swordplay is truly impressive." How did he know about that? This moment's confusion was the time that Bardos chose to strike. Delton successfully deflected the first and second strikes, but the third made contact. The boy didn't mean to kill him, but could have done so just as easily. He had slammed the flat of his blade against Delton's side.

Bardos looked at Delton with what seemed like amusement. "Not bad, Delton. I need to see you in the next session to decide. What about you Miss Frost?" Martha walked forward and Delton handed her the sword. She had barely ever even held a sword. The last time she could remember was when her grandfather had been showing her his cutlass. She had been twelve at the time. This time, Bardos held his sword up with both hands and said, "It is sad isn't it Martha, to lose your grandfather to that accident." She had just been thinking about it. Bardos, who wasn't so startled, had advanced and stopped his blade just before it hit Martha's throat. Martha turned around and went back, wondering how he had known. Alex you're up next."

Alex held his blade high and was planning to use his height against the boy. This time, Bardos tried a different approach, "Hey Alex, have you figured out how to perfect your acoustic weapons yet?" Alex had taken the bait and before he could open his mouth to reply, Bardos had moved in and smashed his elbow into the inventor's gut and brought the blade down towards his neck, before stopping at the last second.

Alan and Andrew had been standing aside, trying to find a weakness. It had become clear. Bardos seemed to have the capability of reading minds and was using it to distract his opponents. Andrew had a plan, it was time to give this kid a taste of his own medicine. They had no chance winning fair and square.

Andrew had been called up next. Before Bardos could begin to speak, Alan let out a scream. All heads turned towards him except one. Bardos called out, "What happened?" Alan replied, "Nothing. I thought I saw a snake. That's all. I'm sorry."

Their attention went back to the fight. Something had changed. Andrew was standing right in front of Bardos. He smashed the hilt of his sword into the boy's gut. The watcher didn't even flinch, but his expression said it. He was defeated. Bardos quickly masked it with a grin and said, "Good job. Alan, its your turn."

Alan stared Bardos right in the eye. Something went wrong. A few seconds later, Alan's expression changed and he dropped the sword at his feet, clutched his chest and kneeled onto the ground. Bardos and the others ran over, screaming his name. He had bought it again. Once he was close enough, Alan struck with his sword. The tip touched Bardos's throat but didn't penetrate his skin. The boy had fallen for his own trick...twice. Alan and Andrew had guessed that this child was no ordinary teenager. The logic behind the strategy was that the boy would expect them to use any strategy just once, thinking that he wouldn't fall for it twice. Instead they had double crossed him by doing what he least expected and fooled him with more or less the same trick.

Patrick was last. He had deciphered Alan and Andrew's strategy, but two times would be the limit. So he had decided to charge ahead and use his sheer mass and force to overpower the boy before he could speak and confuse him.

So as he planned, Patrick Maple stepped into the circle and charged immediately, holding the sword above his head to bring it down with maximum force. What he wasn't realized was that if the boy didn't manage to dodge or defend himself, the strike might kill their only hope of living. Luckily, Bardos was clearly a skilled swordsman and sidestepped at the last moment to escape the slash. Patrick almost fell out of the ring, but he regained his balanced and brought the blade in from the side. Bardos used his own sword to slide along the length of Patrick's. The tip of the boy's sword touched his gut. Patrick Maple was defeated.

After a while, the boy invited them into the hut. It was bigger than it looked. There were seven chairs around a small table. The occupants of six of the chairs sat still, as though the boy had the key to their lives. The truth was, he actually did.

Bardos began like a teacher giving his students their report cards, "Most of you have done rather well. I would also like to tell you that this wasn't to test your sparing abilities, but how it is that you react to certain situations. Now it's time for a little psychological work. A simple question. You may have already been asked this question many times by people as a thought experiment. It is just what you answer. I will give you two options. You must choose one. So is it clear?" The group nodded.

Before Bardos could continue, Alex had a question, "Bardos, what's the reason behind the tests? Why not just let us all in?" The boy hesitated a bit, then told them, "Well there is something coming and we may need two of you to assist us. It's better to let the Harandels explain the entire thing in detail. Well first you must realize that humans are yet to reach their final evolutionary stage. The most evolved of the human race were to be let through the entrance after some tests to make sure that they truly are the right ones. This is all that I am allowed to say. These are the tests to decide that."

Once again several parts of the information being given to them were missing. How were they to understand anything?

So this whole thing had been planned and somehow controlled by the dragons to lure the most evolved humans on the planet to them. The destruction of the island would just give them a motive to get to the entrance. Things were starting to come together but there were still questions, like why the dragons needed the most evolved humans on the planet and which four members would be left behind?

Bardos let a few minutes pass by for the new information to sink in and began his question. "You have to choose between destroying almost every human on the planet in order to save a few who will definitely survive a world-wide catastrophe or you will have to save all humans for now and let them die later."

As the crew thought, Bardos repeated the question a couple of times. I perfectly agree that this sounds extremely childish and hard to believe, but that's what the records say.

Delton was the first to answer, "If I have the power to choose this, it means I have the power to save people if I want to. You didn't mention how many I could save at a time. There is a good chance that I have the power to save everyone. Why should I choose from these options alone?" Bardos nodded, but with a frown and gestured for the next person to answer.

"Save them for now and let fate decide the future," said Martha. "because well…who am I to intervene?"

Patrick agreed with Delton, though he didn't like him, the concept made sense. Meanwhile his brother sided with Martha.

When Alan's turn came, he said, "Andrew and I have a question." Bardos concealed a smile and said, "Go on." Alan asked, "If we let some die now, does it guarantee the survival of the rest?" The boy kept his expression and replied, "Yes." Andrew's reaction to that was, "Then I think we would, unwillingly though…" "Kill humans now for the greater cause to save our species." Alan completed.

It wasn't too clear for now, but Alan and Andrew were the ones who had come out on top in the sword fight. Patrick eventually asked, "Who are the two selected ones?" Bardos was still grinning as he said, "I cannot tell until we get to the entrance. It is at the heart of the island. A mile north of here, but the two businessmen seem promising. I must go alone to bring the key. Go there and wait for my arrival. By the way, the entrance is next to a well. There is only one on the island, so you can't go wrong."

Bardos hadn't told them who it was yet. That statement about the businessmen, however, was in favour of Alan and Andrew. Delton, Patrick, Martha and Alex had been on the verge of giving up, but now a speck of hope shined in the distance. They would head towards it no matter how small it was. This chance, despite the odds, renewed their resolve and now, they actually didn't care. It was either in or out, they would go down fighting. They still had a chance.

Andrew and Alan, the almost probable victors of the challenge were feeling worse than the others, for whom, if they were left behind, almost absolute death was awaiting. Would they prove to be the cause of the death of their friends?

Bardos stood up and walked out of the hut. When the other followed, he had vanished into thin air. They walked slowly back to the camper and strapped themselves to their seats. Delton was driving this time.

Everyone was quiet. Patrick was formulating a plan at the back of his mind. He still had the item that he had received in the package. It could still be used. If this was a literal key that Bardos was bringing, then there could still be a chance. The timing would have to be perfect. He would have to behave normal till then. He would survive if his plan worked out. If it didn't, they would all die. Better one than none.

The camper started driving as the sun started sinking slowly down towards the horizon.

Alan on the other hand was planning too. This involved saving the entire crew. It would be risky and he was playing on a hunch, but there was hope.

In the end it would all come down to who had the better plan, Alan or Patrick. Only time would tell. If only the two of them had shared their plans with the whole crew. Just Alan sharing his plan would have been enough. A life could have been saved.

They were now to heading to the entrance. In the camper, they would have reached within the hour and could have set up camp. That had been the plan. Then again, when had any of their plan's ever gone right?

It was dark when the camper stopped. There were too many trees in front to drive. So they had to go further on foot. "Its just a quarter of a mile more." Alex had informed them. They abandoned their loyal vehicle without which they would have died at the site of their first hurdle. The crew stepped into the darkness with their respective backpacks strapped to their shoulders.

They had barely moved five feet from the door of the camper when...

Chapter 11

TRAPPED INSIDE

The ground caved in and the whole group fell. It was over twenty metres down, but there were a series of vines that slowed their fall. They opened their eyes as they lied on the cold surface of a cave's floor. On the bright side, there hadn't been any stalagmites that could have impaled them.

It took a while for them to get up. Patrick was the first on his feet. He helped the others and they took in their surroundings. They were in a sort of circular room. The walls were smooth and hard rock. The only light was from the moon shining through the hole that had got them there.

None of them had any rope and not a single vine remained, all of them had been ripped apart by the falling crew.

Alan had a torch (flashlight) which refused to work until he banged it against the wall. There also seemed to be a passage branching off to one side.

"What do we do now?" asked Martha. Alex took put a tiny magnetic compass and checked the direction. "That tunnel is heading North and that's the way we want to go. So I say we take that path." Alex said. Patrick realized his hands and stepped to the centre, "Wait a second here guys. We don't know where that leads." Delton was next, "I don't see a better alternative." Alan, Andrew and Martha agreed with him. Patrick bit his lip as they ventured into the unknown. It sounds a bit dramatic, but the events that would follow were on a completely different level.

The beam of light from the torch illuminated what looked like ancient cave drawings. Andrew stepped closer to have a look.

The drawing seemed to represent a sort of battle scene. There were tiny humans around what looked like a dragon with wings and four legs, and a sort of alligator. There was a circle around the dragon. The men standing by the crocodile had spears raised as though in celebration.

Was this a scene that they had witnessed? The answer was lost with time. Or was it?

The crew eventually hit a dead end. Though, that wall was made of some glittering metal. It radiated its own light but was just as cool as the rocks.

"What do you think this is?" enquired Delton. "Is it…is it the entrance?" Andrew shook his head, "No. Don't you remember? The entrance is next to a well and I can't see a single well anywhere close."

Their discussion was interrupted by a screech further up the tunnel. For a second they were of the glow elephants, but one couldn't possibly fit into the tiny space. This had to be something different.

A few seconds later, small, one metre tall creatures with only three legs came bolting towards the shining wall. They were small, but the sight of hooked claws and teeth were menacing.

Alan thought it to be awkward that this didn't surprise him, but after the events of the past forty-eight hours, he doubted that much could surprise him now.

There were hundreds of these little animals, piling up at that end of the tunnel. The whole night was spent by the crew, hiding in the same spot. None of them had slept even for a minute, due to the fear of being discovered. They found a spot to hide and squeezed in.

Sunlight finally entered the tunnel through the holes on the ceiling. The darkness that had been their cloak for so long was slipping away. Just as a beam of white light touched the metal, the creatures started squealing. The sound was not too different from the one the glow elephants had made.

The metal seemed to vibrate at first, following the squeals. The vibration soon turned to violent shaking and the metal seemed to melt into a liquid. It fell onto the ground with a splash. The silver liquid seemed to be trying to regain its form, but was held down for some reason. The horde of monsters bolted to the other side with surprising speed, coordination and agility for a creature with three legs.

The crew stayed where they were, resisting the urge to get out of the claustrophobic space where they had been crammed into for several hours. The moment that the last of them was through, they stopped their little song and the solid metal gate reformed almost instantaneously.

The next hour or so had been spent by the crew planning a way out. "The metal probably reacts to the sound they make." Martha said. No one had a better theory, so they decided to act on the basis of what Miss Frost thought was most probably the truth.

Patrick rubbed his hands together. He reached into his backpack and produced a tiny handgun-like device. Alex looked stunned, "How did you get one?" He was referring to one of his acoustic weapons that had been disbanded due to their tendency to blow up in the face of their wielder. They weren't to be sold until the problem had been resolved. "We can talk about that later, but for now, do you think we can blast our way through." Andrew shook his head, "No, it might attract the attention of the creatures that left. For all we know, they could be on the other side of that door or at least close enough to this place to hear an explosion." Alan then said, "Plus, if it turns to a liquid at a particular frequency, we don't know how it might react to a different one." "I have a better idea." said Delton, "Maybe the creatures will come back out and if they use the same frequency of sound, we theoretically can record it on the blaster and open the door once they're gone." Alex admitted, "He's right. The device can record sounds and analyse frequencies too. Though, that isn't exactly safe. Well, what are the odds?" The question had been rhetorical, but Patrick answered, "Probably fifty-fifty." Not too reliable but it was all they had.

It was nearly 11'o clock before they heard the footsteps. The crew went back to their hiding spot. They had predicted that the animals might return from the inside. Instead five more came from the other direction.

Alex prepared the device by putting it on record mode. The squeals sounded through the tunnel again. The weapon analysed every rise and fall in the pitch of sound. A green light flashed in the screen in the handle just as the door solidified again.

The group stepped out in the open. Delton held the blaster in his hand. There was a good chance that it might blow up, but he seemed confident. The one who's idea it was, pressed the trigger and an exact acoustic replica of the squeal had been created. They kept it on till all of them were through.

They had entered another long passageway. It lead to a large circular room. The room had a rough diameter of five-hundred feet with a boulder covering the next passage. Patrick swore. They tried to push it aside, but it was too heavy. Alex moved closer to the boulder and pointed out that it was attached to a sort of counterweight on the other side of the wall. Something had to be done and fast. Time was running out, they had to reach the entrance. Then again, there was the more imminent chance of the creatures returning.

There was a sudden tremor, or at least that's what it felt like. Some rocks feel from the ceiling of the room. The crew barely managed to dodge the missiles trying to kill them. Once it stopped, their was a gaping hole in the roof and a cage fell through. It was tied at its corners to some unseen support within the hole.

Though the worst of their worries weren't done yet. The cage held one large glowing creature. It looked the same as the ones near the river that they had seen. That incident seemed like an eternity ago. It was a miracle that the thin ropes held the weight of the creature. Then they noticed it. The cage was slowly descending. They had to get out of there, now.

Alex was struggling to figure out the working of the boulder. He decided to look at it from another point of view. How would a three legged creature open that door. Then he saw it. A small opening, like a key hole was cut into the rock on one side. Perhaps the tail, or one of the creature's legs could be used like a key to activate the mechanism.

Right on cue, three of the three-legged animals emerged from the passage that they had entered through. It turned out that they in fact were capable of making sounds other than that squeal. They hissed and two of them stepped forward, as the other edged towards their right flank. There were a few bamboo sticks near the boulder which had been left over from the construction of the door. It was a mystery as to who had built it. One of many. Alan, Delton and Andrew grabbed one each. Martha had taken the gun which Patrick had tried to shoot Alan with earlier. There had been only two bullets left and she hadn't wished to waste them, but now was the time. Patrick retrieved his brother's acoustic blaster which still wasn't recommended by the crew. Though, considering their current situation, that might have just given them the edge.

The one approaching from the side attacked first. It was neatly disposed of by Alan, who whacked it aside with a wave of his new staff. The poor creature hit the ground with a thud.

Martha fired a shot at one of the two left. It dodged skilfully. For a second, her eyes strayed to the cage of the Crenobel. It was much closer to the ground than before.

The two three-legged monsters raced towards them. Delton stepped forward and thrust the end of his stick into its open mouth. It stumbled back but was still standing.

The other one used the crew's temporary amazement at Delton's skill, to pounce at Andrew. Patrick knocked it right out of the air with a high frequency sound wave. They looked at each other and nodded. It conveyed a simple message, *Thank you,* and, *It's okay.*

"Bring one of the unconscious animals over here." Alex yelled across the room. They didn't understand why, but Martha and Alan ran over to one of the creatures. They each grabbed a leg and began dragging it to the boulder. Goodness, it was heavy.

What had happened was that Alex had found a small hole next to the boulder, shaped like the creature's claw. He figured that it would have to be placed in the slot to make the door open.

Meanwhile Patrick fired a few experimental shots with his weapon. The light on the screen turned red, warning him that the device was getting overheated. He had to stop.

Now only a few bamboo sticks stood between them and the animal. It took a running leap towards Andrew. This time he was prepared. He fell flat on the floor and smashed the bamboo stick into the thing's gut as it sailed through the air above him.

Alan and Martha reached the boulder. Alex helped them place its paw on the indent. They expected a click and the boulder to move, but nothing happened.

Just a second later, they heard ropes snapping. The cage fell to the floor a few hundred years away. It had been high enough for the cage to break on impact and low enough for the glow elephant to survive the fall.

The others re-joined Alan, Alex and Martha at the boulder. "What happened? Why isn't it open?" asked Delton. "I don't know," spat Alex, completely distraught. "I...I don't know."

The Crenobel stopped glowing, just like back in the forest. It stood up and charged at them. Before anyone did anything Andrew yelled, "Wait, stay where you are. We can use it to smash the boulder open." Patrick considered using the acoustic blaster, but the display still blinked red. An explosion might kill them all.

The boulder smashing would also make quite a commotion and the creatures may be right on the other side. They might as well have used the blaster in the first place. Now this was their only hope. As usual their chances of survival were low, but they had to try.

The crew had been hoping to never encounter a Crenobel again…or at least not by themselves. They could really use a massive, killer dragon right now.

The massive animal's eyes seemed to shimmer with bloodlust. It seemed to take an eternity for the monster to run towards them. Andrew knew that he had to time this perfectly or the lot of them would catch a one way trip to afterlife.

As the Crenobel drew closer, Alan said with unconcealed panic in his voice, "Andrew." He replied with just one word, "Wait." The Crenobel was almost upon them when he screamed, "Jump." The group jumped, four to the left and the other two to the right.

The Crenobel, however, wasn't so lucky. It slammed into the boulder, reducing it to rubble and knocking itself out.

Though this incident sounds long, it happened in a matter of seconds. The aftermath of this was rather spectacular.

The boulder had been, in every sense, destroyed. The three-legged creatures were nowhere to be seen. They had probably run away to save themselves. The crew couldn't believed their luck. Bright sunlight shown through where the boulder had been and there were no creatures on the other side.

The crew carefully ventured into the open, their weapons at the ready in case they found any more inhabitants of the island lurking around. "I know I'm a biologist and its my job, but I think I've had enough of animals." said Martha. The group shared a brief laugh at that comment.

The sun was directly overhead, which meant it was close to noon and they had barely a few hours before the island was destroyed. They were all utterly exhausted. None of them had got even a bit of sleep the previous night. Their eyes were bloodshot and swollen. Their limbs were tired and they felt like collapsing, but they couldn't give up.

Well each of them knew that Alan and Andrew were the ones who would survive, but the watcher had not told them that himself. This meant that they had a chance to live. Its funny what a human might be willing to go through to live.

As they forged on, towards the heart of the island, Patrick began to doubt himself. Was he really doing the right thing? Was his life worth killing his fellow crew members? It had to be. Anyway he had come too far and it was too late to change his mind now. The truth was that he could. There was another way, a better way to live.

Alan on the other hand was thinking of something else. He hoped this whole thing was a nightmare and he could wake up. He tried several tricks shown in movies to convince himself that something good would eventually occur. It was irritating, being constantly reminded that he was in real life and this adventure may not exactly have a happy ending.

The only thing Alan relied on was his own plan. In the end it would succeed, but at a cost.

At the end of the adventure Alan would look back to this moment and curse himself for not taking the right decisions. There were so many ways that he could have saved all his friends. Alas! No one can alter past events, except perhaps the Harandels and the governing forces, but all in good time.

The crew had all this going on through their minds as Delton who was in front of the group came to a halt. He spread out his arms, as though shielding his friends. The astrophysicist turned his head from right to left and said, "Did you hear that sound?"

Alex grabbed his head with both hands. He was experiencing that feeling again. Every time something bad happened to them, there would be this question which almost seemed to trigger the events. For example, before running into the pirates, "What are those lights?" Or their first encounter with the Crenobels, "What are those?" The horror seemed to start almost right after the question.

Alex's intuition wasn't mistaken. Just a few seconds after Delton had asked the question, the bushes in front parted and this time, it wasn't Bardos.

Chapter 12

ALPHA PREDATOR

The Tenebris Chorés expedition crew now stared into the face of a humanoid creature. It was the size of a three storey building and smelled like sweaty socks, dipped in rotten eggs and rolled in dung. As gross as it sounds, that's almost exactly how it smelled.

The monster was bald and reminded Martha of a troll described in ancient legends. It was dressed in a sort of handmade cloth with countless stains. Some of which resembled blood stains. Actually, most of them.

The entire crew took a step back. All their instincts told them to run, but this creature could catch them with ease.

As the monster stepped forwards and into the sunlight pepping through the gap in the branches, the crew noticed that it had a blue hue to its skin. To their great surprise it said, "Food?" Alan didn't understand whether it was a question or a statement, but either way, when the troll said food, it was definitely referring to them. Not good.

Someone had to act fast and this time, Patrick Maple decided that it was up to him. He drew his acoustic blaster. The display was now green. He aimed it at the creature. "Patrick, don't." screamed Delton. If only he would listen.

The next few seconds were a blur of action. Firstly the blaster went off target and blew a tree to smithereens. The relatively tame monster leaped back in shock. For a brief moment the crew thought it would turn tail and run. Instead it turned towards them and slashed at the ground with massive talons. Fortunately the crew dodged it. The creature said again, "Food." This time it was more certain.

Alan and Patrick had jumped away in the same direction. Once they stood up, Alan grabbed the geologist's shoulder and yelled, "Are you out of your mind? You fired at it when it was just standing there, doing nothing. Now look at it." Patrick may have caused triggered the creature's sudden rage, but his intentions had been genuine, "Get your hand off, Sawner. If you could do better, why didn't you?" Alan decided that there was no point arguing, the damage was done. He ran to help the others.

Patrick spat on the floor. He had had his doubts, but now he was sure. Alan deserved what he was about to do.

The crew dodged several slashes from the troll. Soon they realized that the creature was not too good at depth perception.

It was just starting to look like they might get away, when the troll broke a branch off a large tree and swung it towards Alex like a club. He yelped and managed to jump over the it like a skipping rope.

Alex sighed and looked at the other, "Now that was a close one, huh?" The moment he completed the sentence, the troll's makeshift club slammed into his back. The force of the impact knocked the wind out of his lungs.

The troll hefted the formerly conscious Alex Maple and slung him onto its back. This was when they snapped. They were facing odds that no human had ever faced. Creatures that supposedly didn't exist had almost killed them. They had come so far due to luck, but it was sure to run out eventually.

Alan and Andrew felt miserable. Though they didn't admit it, they were confident that the two of them were the ones chosen to live. They just pretended that everyone had an equal chance to keep the others going. Andrew had hesitated at first, but Alan assured him that he could save the others. Though he didn't disclose his plan.

So now that they had come this far, was it alright to give up. Could they just let fate decide for them? Did they have a choice?

The next victim would be Martha. She still had the gun, which they had stolen from the pirates. She drew the weapon and fired. The bullet hit its mark. The creature dropped its club and clutched its right eye. The four others thought it was over. Perhaps the creature would be disabled long enough for them to escape.

They sidestepped towards where Martha was standing, not for a second taking their eyes off the troll.

"Nice shot.", commented Delton. "Thanks." replied Martha. Patrick was in a bit of a hurry, "Yeah, good job, but can we save it for later? First, let's figure out how to get my brother down from there and put as much distance between us and this thing."

Andrew was about to suggest using a vine to try and make the monster fall, when the troll let out a deafening roar.

The troll had recovered from the shock. Though one of its eyes was blinded, it could still see. It smashed the ground where Delton, Martha and Andrew were standing. They were safe…in a sense. The troll's hand hadn't crushed them, but had pinned them to the ground. Using its other hand, the monster picked them up, turned around and walked away.

Meanwhile, Alan and Patrick were safe. They had been hiding behind a tree and luckily the troll wasn't too good at remembering how many of them had been there.

The two remaining men sat on the ground. There wasn't much they could do. Alan was the first to break the silence, "Hey Patrick, I'm sorry for screaming at you back there. I knew you were trying to shoot the troll with the blaster. It wasn't your fault that it went crazy and started attacking." Patrick Maple didn't expect to hear this from Alan. Was he apologizing?

Guilt filled Patrick's heart. How could he have possibly thought to do that to his friend? He had judged him in a few seconds. He had barely given any thought to the possibility that he might not have meant it.

Silence returned. About half an hour passed before Patrick mustered the courage to say, "Alan, Bardos had said that two of us would be let through right? Well, let's face it, there isn't much of a chance that the others might possibly escape. Why don't we just move on and find the entrance?"

Alan was taken aback by Patrick's statement. He said, "Patrick, are you saying that we should abandon them. Right now they're probably praying for us to rescue them."

They indeed were. The troll had thrown each of them over its shoulder and was walking through an endless catacomb of tunnels. Andrew was kept thinking, *Not more tunnels.*

Patrick didn't exactly enjoy the idea of battling a thirty foot troll, even if it meant looking like the hero. "For all we know they might already be dead."

Alan was outraged. How could someone be this selfish? He stood up and said, "I don't know about you Patrick, but I'm going to find my friends." He turned around and began running in the direction that the troll had gone.

Patrick slapped his forehead. As much as he wanted to increase his odds of getting through the entrance, he didn't want to travel through the forest alone.

The geologist stood up and bolted after Alan unto the woods.

It may sound difficult to look for a troll which is relatively small compared to a large island, but Alan and Patrick were having no problems. The stench from the monster was so strong that if they closed their eyes, they would almost swear that it was right in front if them. Apart from that, the troll had smashed several trees on its way.

The two men eventually reached a cave. "Do we have to go inside?" asked Patrick. Alan just nodded and stepped in.

The troll smelled bad, but the cave was in a completely different league. Patrick thought he was about to faint and stumbled on his way in. The two of them cupped their hands over their noses and. tried their best to breathe as little as possible.

Just a few feet into the tunnel, it split into two. The picked the one on the right and kept heading on. Further down the tunnel split again and the took the one on the right again. Alan had said, "If we take the tunnel on the right each time, we won't have to bother ourselves with choosing which tunnel to take, just in case we have to leave in a hurry." "True.", Patrick replied.

On the bright side the, at least the place wasn't booby trapped.

Twenty-four right turns later, they hit a dead end. This was depressing. The ran back to the previous split in the tunnel and took the one on the left. No luck.

They retraced their steps and tried each left turn. Finally on their fifteenth try, they entered a cavern. A loud roar sounded as the troll came into view. "What now?" asked Patrick. "Look for the others." replied Alan.

It wasn't too tough. The place had nothing except a few, rusty plane parts.

The other crew members soon came into view. They were tied with vines, but looked intact. Alex was conscious again, but he was as pale as a ghost. "Okay," said Alan, "we sneak around those plane wrecks, using them as cover. Let's try to find a sharp piece of metal from the parts lying there to cut the vines." Patrick nodded reluctantly and followed Alan.

The two men crawled towards their fellow crew members. The troll turned around and they jumped behind a broken wing of a plane for cover. Patrick was sweating and began to realize what a bad idea this was. He should have just let Alan go to his death alone. By now he would have made it to the entrance. He whispered, "Alan, if we die here and there is an afterlife, I'm going to kill you again there."

Andrew was sure that there was no hope for him and the other three. Alan and Patrick had obviously done the logical thing and headed to the entrance. Sooner of later the troll was going to eat them up and use their bones as toothpicks. He soon regretted the thought about using bones as toothpicks, now he was feeling nauseous.

Andrew turned his head around and couldn't believe his eyes. He was sure that the lack of sleep and fatigue was playing tricks on his mind.

The troll had turned away. Patrick and Alan continued their progress towards the rest of the crew. Alan noticed Andrew looking at him and smiled. Then he mouthed the words, *hang on.*

Andrew knew this had to be real, whispered to the other, "Hey, everyone, quick...look here." Six more eyes turned towards Alan and he nodded his head. They were saved...for the time being.

As they edged closer, Alan noticed a rather sharp stone lying on the ground next to him. He picked it up and placed it in his pocket.

Finally they reached their friends. Alan cut the other free of their bonds. They rubbed their wrists and ankles. "We thought you'd gone to the entrance. You're wasting your time on us." Alan checked his watch. It was 4'o clock. The sun would set approximately at 6'o clock, which meant they had two hours to go before the deadline to open the entrance would pass.

"We can argue about that later, for now, let's try to get out of here." They turned around and started crawling back to the mouth of the cavern.

The crew froze as the troll turned around. Its hand reached to the spot where Delton, Alex, Martha and Andrew had been. It tapped around as though that would bring its missing meal back. "Food where?" it yelled.

It ran around frantically and eventually got dizzy, crashing to the floor. The scene was almost hilarious, like an animated kid's show.

"That's our cue." said Andrew. They were heading back to the main tunnel when Patrick's hand bumped into a plane's propeller. One of the three blades fell off and hit the stone floor.

The noise echoed through the room and the troll snapped out of its daze. It yelled pretty much the only word it knew, "Food." Though how it learnt the word remains a mystery.

The troll turned it's head around frantically and it wasn't too long before they were discovered. There was no use crawling now. The crew stood up and ran. Alan and Patrick were in front because they we're the only one who remembered the path to the exit.

The troll was fast for its size and was catching up, but suddenly it disappeared. The crew finally slowed down, still panting.

At last the crew saw light shining through the exit, but almost immediately it was gone as the troll appeared before them. They had no choice except to turn and run, which they did.

The troll instead smashed it's foot onto the ground. The tunnel rumbled and the section of the tunnel ceiling in front of them fell to the floor.

The crew knew that they were trapped, but for some reason, kept running. They barely made it a hundred yards when Alan tripped and fell. "Get up Alan, get up." Andrew screamed.

He just couldn't go on any further. "I give up.", he yelled, staring at the ceiling. A tear rolled down the side of his cheek. He had been hiding his emotions, behaving strong for his crew, but this was it. He gave up to fate. He ignored the voices of his friends and closed his eyes, preparing himself for the death that would come in a matter of seconds.

Andrew and the others could do nothing but stare. They watched the troll roar in triumph as it brought its massive fist down on Alan.

As Alan awaited the end, he heard a voice in his head, *Alan... don't give up. You have come very close to victory. Just fight a little longer.*

Alan was sure that this voice belonged to the red Harandel he had seen in Jakarta. It was warm and soothing, just like it had been when he had first heard it.

The moment he heard the voice, strength seemed to rush back into his tired muscles. His mind was cleared and he could think straight once again. The Harandel was right. He had come too far to give up now.

Alan opened his eyes, only to see the troll's hand rushing towards him and then suddenly disappear.

In reality, Patrick had shot the troll with his acoustic blaster, just before it crushed Alan. The sound waves had sent it sailing through the air.

The troll had never been attacked by any other creature in its whole life. Anything that could send the troll flying, had to be stronger than it.

The monster which had landed twenty feet away, got up and ran out of the tunnel.

It took poor Alan a few seconds to process all this.

The crew gathered around him. "Are you okay Alan?" asked Alex. His reply was, "Huh?" Patrick knelt down, grabbed his shoulders and shook Alan violently. "Hey, are you okay? What happened to you?"

The shaking had helped Alan snap out of the shock. "Sorry," he said, "I was a bit…depressed. Thanks for shooting it." A bit depressed was an understatement. In fact, he was on the verge of hysteria.

The crew helped Alan up and the six of them, reunited once again, walked into the open.

They now had barely an hour and a half to sunset.

The crew kept forging ahead towards the centre of the island. Soon enough, they Walked into a clearing. In the centre was a well and a stone tower.

The crew almost jumped with relief. They had made it. They were at the entrance.

Now it was all up to the watcher to show up. With this relief, also came fear. Bardos was going to tell them which of the crew members had been chosen to survive. What would be the fate of the others.

Chapter 13

REUNION

The expedition crew's reunion with the watcher wasn't what they had expected. For starters, Bardos the watcher has emerged into clearing, looking as though he had been rammed by a truck. His clothes had holes in them and were singed.

The boy himself was in no better condition. His skin was covered with scratches and bruises. The was a particularly nasty cut above his left eyebrow.

Alan, Andrew and the others had been sitting on piles of dry leaves that had been lying on the ground. When they saw Bardos coming, they had rushed to keep him from falling.

Delton didn't understand what could have happened to Bardos. They had faced him in combat and he had been toying with them. He had just been trying to choose the worthiest of the crew and had barely used his full potential. The boy himself was definitely not any ordinary human. If the Harandels had entrusted him with the key of the entrance, Bardos must posses some supernatural powers. Delton silently promised himself, never to run into whatever did this to Bardos. A promise which he would soon have to break.

Alex asked, "Bardos, what did this to you?" The watcher replied, but his voice was weak and raspy, "A troll...possessed by Antrosel." Possessed? Now there were ghosts on this island. Just what they needed.

"Wha...what do you mean 'possessed by Antrosel?'" asked Andrew. Bardos coughed and replied, "A troll possessed by a being called Antrosel attacked me. It took the key to the entrance. Without it, no one will survive, not even me."

This last sentence had quite an effect on the crew. The only thing that had kept them going so far with unwavering courage was the small chance that they might survive, but now The key was gone, taken by a troll possessed by some ghost.

"So now you're telling us, we're going to die because you couldn't fight off a troll?" yelled Patrick. He said 'fight off a troll' like 'fight of a cat', but he had earned the right to say so. After all, he had done so himself.

Martha ignored Patrick and said, "Bardos, who's Antrosel?" The boy coughed again and said, "I can't say much...it is up for the Harandels to tell the two chosen ones, but the only thing I can tell you is that Antrosel is a powerful and ancient being who can control other creatures." Delton said next, "So what do we do now? Just wait for the island to blow up?"

Alex checked his watch, an hour left for sunset. Alan was next to speak, "Is there no other way Bardos?" The watchers eyes seemed to brighten just a bit. He replied, "Antrosel isn't too far away, in fact he's in the same set of tunnels you escaped from. The key is in that cave. If you can retrieve it, there is a chance. Its the last trial Alan, complete it and you can be saved."

The last trial? There was something about this that bothered Alan. If this was to be the last trial, were the previous troubles they had faced also just tests? He decided to put it aside for later.

Andrew was glad that they had escaped the troll earlier. They had done so only due to its stupidity, but they had to face it again now. This time it was possessed by an intelligent being. Strength and intelligence together would make quite a deadly combination.

If this monster had almost killed Bardos, what assurance did they have that they could possibly defeat it?

The rest of the crew were pondering over the same idea.

"We'll go," Alan said and turned to the others, "if it's the only way, we'll have to go. There is no choice. Look at how far we've come. We fought pirates, escaped from glow elephants, three-legged dogs and defeated a troll, just fight on a little bit longer."

The pep talk didn't work as well as Alan would have wanted it to. Patrick had crashed back down on the pile of leaves and said, "Oh what's the point? Even if we had the key, Andrew and you would be saved. We know Bardos chose the two of you."

Though he didn't reveal it, Patrick was eager to get the key, but didn't want to risk his life. If the key was returned, his plan would work and he would live. He hoped that Alan would oppose him and go retrieve the key anyway.

"I didn't say that. I haven't told you who have been chosen to pass through the entrance." said Bardos. Andrew was next to speak, "We can keep that for later. I'm going with Alan, who's with me?"

Alex, Patrick and Martha walked over to where Alan and Andrew were. The five of them looked down at Patrick. He stood up and joined them. Though he acted reluctant about going, he was buzzing with excitement. There was a chance…a small chance to live, but a chance nonetheless.

"We'll get the key Bardos, hang on." said Delton. "Wait," said Bardos, "the key is not like any that you may expect. It a cube, carved from stone attached to a golden chain." "Thank you Bardos. We'll remember." Alex assured him.

Then the crew walked back in the direction they had come from. Forty-five minutes was all they had before sunset. Forty-five minutes to save themselves from destruction.

As they walked Alan, knelt down, pretending to tie his shoelaces. Just as Andrew walked by, Alan grabbed his wrist. He stood up and pulled Andrew aside.

"What's wrong Alan?" Andrew asked, concerned for his friend. He didn't want Alan to have a nervous breakdown like he had in the tunnel. Alan told Andrew his plan. If they managed to get back alive with the key, Bardos would tell them who would be let through. Up to that point, Alan and the others had assumed that the survivors would be chosen based on the tests that he had given them earlier, but if their other encounters on the island would be taken into account, it could be anyone. The plan had been for Alan to refuse to enter unless the safety of the others was guaranteed.

Now that the decision wasn't clear, the plan might not work. What if Alan and Andrew weren't chosen at all?

Andrew took this new information in. He said, "You've changed Alan." Alan shrugged and replied, "We have to adapt to survive. Anyway, if either of us get through, stick to the plan." Andrew nodded. Then they quickly returned to the group. When Martha asked them what happened, they simply lied that they had been praying.

None of the crew spoke as they approached the tunnel. It looked the same as it had when they left, except now it was glowing red.

The crew entered, afraid to even touch the walls of the tunnel. They found a passage to the left which curved around the main tunnel and merged with it again. They used this passage as the ceiling had been collapsed in the tunnel by the troll on their way out. It was also probably the same tunnel that the troll had used to get ahead of them on their previous visit.

Finally they reached the same cavern in which they had been earlier.

This time it was filled with the hundreds of the three-legged creatures they had seen earlier. The troll looked completely different now. It had a tail which had a claw at its end. It had grown horns and stood on all four limbs. Its head seemed elongated and looked like a jackal's, except for the ears. Now it looked less humanoid and more like an animal.

Alan's jaw dropped in surprise as the troll began to say something other than food, "Creatures of this island, do not forget who created you. Our lord has returned. He requires a new form, a stronger form. Prove your loyalties and join us."

What was Antrosel/the troll even talking about? Where did he learn English and did the creatures even understand English?

Martha interrupted Alan's thoughts by saying, "What is that troll talking about? Their lord?" Alan was glad that he wasn't the only one who'd heard it speaking.

Alex was pretty analytical and could generally find a logical explanation for most things, but this island was too much to comprehend, he was definitely regretting this expedition. He looked at the others and said, "We can discus that later. Concentrate on finding the key."

Sooner than they expected, the crew noticed the cube tied to a golden chain around the troll's neck.

Now how were they going to get the key? It was with Antrosel who supposedly had hundreds of those deadly three-legged creatures under his command.

Unexpectedly Antrosel turned to look at the exact spot where the crew had been crouching. He stood up on two legs and roared. Then he said, "Alan Sawner, Andrew Briston, Delton Kraig, Patrick Maple, Martha Frost and Alex Maple...welcome. I have been looking forward to this meeting for a long time. Come out, don't hide."

This latest development struck fear into the crew's hearts. There was something about Antrosel's voice that seemed to take over their minds. They walked into the open, completely terrified. They were in a sort of trance. Thy had no clue why they had obeyed Antrosel. At the time it seemed to be the right thing to do.

Antrosel laughed and it was unlike any laugh they had ever heard. It was cold and heartless. "You have many questions, don't you?"

The crew members were too frightened to speak.

Eventually Andrew mustered the courage to say, "Give us the key and we'll be on our way." Antrosel laughed again and said, "Andrew, what you must understand is that your planet will soon be destroyed and there is no hope for you humans. Even of you do take the key, it will be of no use. Once your planet is destroyed, even the Harandels cannot defend you against our lord."

116

None of them wanted to believe a word that Antrosel said, but they felt he was telling the truth. Though the meaning of the words weren't too clear as they were in the dark when it came to mystical lords destroying planets.

As far as they understood, even if two of the crew were allowed through the entrance and saved, it wouldn't matter as the entire planet would be destroyed. Somehow after destroying the planet, this lord would be stronger than the Harandels and would kill the two crew members anyway.

Technically the two people who would be saved now were only postponing their deaths.

Alan was getting tired of this. He decided to say, "If it doesn't matter whether we get the key or not, just give it to us." Antrosel replied, "You amuse me Alan Sawner. It would be quite pleasurable to use you as a jester, perhaps. Its a pity that the lord ordered the destruction of every human in existence. Which includes you. I cannot take chances when it comes to the lord's orders."

The crew's situation was not improving and their time was running out, half an hour for sunset.

Antrosel was losing his patience. It was time to get rid of these pests, "Show your loyalty to Lord Shanarkus. Attack!"

At last they knew this person's name. Exactly what that was supposed to mean, was still a mystery.

Alan had anticipated that this would happen. He had taken the acoustic blaster from Patrick's backpack and has set it to the widest possible range.

The moment the wave of monsters began running towards them, Alan fired. The force was unbelievable. Even Antrosel couldn't hold his ground.

Antrosel willed the troll's body to stand up and said, "Impressive, but not good enough." More monsters charged at them. Alan shot wave after wave of monsters.

The others tried to be of as much help as they could. They threw rocks, plane propellers and anything else they could find at the creatures. Yet they were no closer to getting the key cube that they were ten minutes ago.

"Its hopeless humans. You cannot fight all of them off." bellowed Antrosel. "Alan, as much as I hate to admit it, he's right." said Delton. "Alan if you keep firing that thing, its going to explode." "Thats exactly what I want" replied Alan. Alex stared at him with a puzzled expression.

It took him a while, but Patrick understood what Alan was planning to do, "You're going to use it as a grenade." Alan smiled in his direction and replied, "Exactly."

The display of the A-95 Acoustic Blaster turned yellow and displayed the number six. This indicated that Alan had six shots left before the device exploded.

Alan took aim to fire again, but was blinded by a flash of green light. Swirling green light seemed to take the shape of a being.

The creatures froze, looked up at the light and began to howl.

Antrosel lost his composure. He seemed terrified. The previously terrifying monster was now not so scary. He pressed his back against the cave wall and took deep breaths.

Antrosel stared at the light and gasped, "It can't be you... you were imprisoned." A voice replied. It seemed to come from all direction, as though they were in the throat of some gigantic animal, "If Shanarkus can escape the abyss, so can I. Do not forget your position Antrosel."

The light then seemed to condense into a ball. It radiated light and heat like a miniature sun. It then exploded in all directions. It spread throughout the cavern. Just before it could reach Antrosel, he lifted his hands in front of him, as though to protect himself and he was suddenly enveloped in a sphere of silver light.

The creatures however were helpless. The green blast vaporised them. Where they had been standing, were now signed black marks in the ground.

The crew closed their eyes and instinctively covered their faces with their arms, but the light just passed over them, leaving them unharmed. In fact they weren't just unharmed, they felt stronger.

118

Miraculously the cube had disappeared from Antrosel's neck and appeared on the ground before the crew. Andrew picked it up.

The crew looked at Antrosel who still looked a bit confused or it could have just been his usual expression. It's tough to say when it comes to a troll possessed by an ancient psychic being with altered facial features.

A look at the humans in the cavern seemed to help Antrosel recover. He looked at them and yelled, "Don't think you're saved yet humans. You still have to defeat me."

As usual the crew had only one choice, to turn and run for their lives.

Chapter 14

TOUGH DECISIONS

Running through a maze of tunnels, chased by a troll wasn't Alan's idea of having a good day.

The main tunnel had collapsed, so the crew took the same passageway that they had entered through.

"I see the exit." said Alex, still running. The green light in the cavern had given them an energy boost, but they were running out of breath. Antrosel was getting closer. Alan fired a shot from his acoustic blaster which had little effect. Five more shots for the blaster to overload.

Alan realized that they had to stay inside the tunnel when the blaster exploded, they would die too. He came to a skidding halt and fired three shots in quick succession. Antrosel couldn't handle the continuous blows and crashed to the floor.

Alan had two shots left. Then it struck him. He would only kill the troll, but not Antrosel if this plan succeeded. Could Antrosel possibly possess one of them? Well at least Antrosel wouldn't have as much power as the troll if he possessed one of the crew.

The crew started running again. The others got out of the cave, but Alan remained inside. Patrick called out to him, "Alan, come on, let's go." "Wait." Alan replied, "If we go out It will just follow us."

Antrosel stood up again, now walking leisurely towards them. Alan was confused at first, then looked at the sky. It was turning orange. Alex noticed it too and looked at his watch. They had ten more minutes.

Alan fired one more shot. The blaster was vibrating in his hands. He pressed a few buttons on the blaster. The next shot would be fired in ten seconds. He ten threw it at Antrosel's feet.

"Is this a mark of surrender human?" asked Antrosel as he picked up the baster which seemed tiny in his hands.

The last shot fired, which made Antrosel stumble and fall fat on his back. Alan turned and ran. The explosion was defeating. White hot flames engulfed the troll's body. It roared in pain as the tunnel roof crumbled down on the troll. Alan almost felt sad for the creature. It had been possessed by Antrosel and couldn't help it. It didn't deserve that fate.

The troll's body glowed red and its features returned to the way they had been when the crew had seen it for the first time. Its tail disappeared. So did its horns. Its face returned to normal (in a sense) and its lips seemed to curl into a smile. If the troll had meant to smile, it was probably out of joy that it was finally rid of the creature that had taken over it's mind.

Then for a second a ghostly image of the troll, much smaller in size appeared before the crew at the exit. It spoke, "Alan Sawner...you may think you have defeated me, but you have merely defeated my host. Soon you will have to face me, the real me. Sooner than you think."

The crew expected something to happen. For the ghost to try and attack them, but it merely seemed to fade away.

The six of them just stood there, each thinking about something different. Alan took charge once again, "Hurry, we barely have a few minutes left."

The first time that they had gone to the entrance from the cave, it had taken them half an hour. They had been walking and didn't know the way, but now they managed to squeeze it down to ten minutes.

As they ran through the woods, they realized that they had, in fact, overcome unbelievable obstacles. Every time the odds had been against them, but they had kept going. It surprised each of them, what a human can do to survive. Yet it wasn't certain. As the moment drew closer, it almost didn't matter. They reasoned that everyone's death would come one day or the other. Perhaps it would be best of accept their fate and be happy for their friends who would continue. For all they cared, they had proven themselves to their hearts.

The last rays of sunlight were on the verge disappearing as the broke into the clearing, desperate for breath. Bardos had recovered from his injuries, but still looked exhausted. He greeted them with a smile, "Alan, you did it. Good job."

The crew was too tensed to reply. Patrick couldn't wait any longer, he asked, "Who is it Bardos? Who are the ones you have chosen?"

It was the moment of truth. Bardos smiled and said, "Alan and Andrew." The other crew members nodded. It had always been clear. Patrick was about to begin the first phase of his plan, he said, "Then why didn't you tell us Bardos? You could have just told us that when you tested us by that hut. You didn't have to tempt us, give us hope and later snatch it away in such an act of cruelty."

The watcher looked guilty. He faced the crew and said, "I admit…it was cruel. I had chosen Alan and Andrew at the test, but the rest of you were almost equally promising. I couldn't decide with just two tests. I had to test you more. Thus the other encounters you had in the island had to be observed and each of you had to be evaluated. Forgive me, but this is my final decision."

The crew surged towards Bardos, their faces twisted with anger. The watcher knew what to do. He stamped hard on the ground and blue sparks flew in all directions. The spell had the crew walking away and sitting down in no time.

Bardos took the key and walked over to the column of stone. He slid the cube into a slot just as the sky turned black. The moon was hidden behind some clouds. He began chanting something under his breath. Alan and Andrew were standing aside, talking in hushed tones.

The four others whose lives were doomed, sat by the column. Martha was in tears. Alex refused to respond to anyone. Patrick and Delton were the only ones talking. "Patrick," Delton had said, "I know you don't like me." This statement had caught Patrick by surprise. "You think I stole your position as most renowned scientist in the world. You think I did it on purpose, but you're wrong. If anything, you were my inspiration. Your Mars project inspired me to do something big. It brought me out of my fear that I may become a failure. Thanks to you, I have had such a good life. If I ever did anything to offend you, I'm sorry Mr Maple."

Patrick was experiencing quite a few emotions, mainly guilt, but also surprise and a sense of respect. Delton was a good person, how could Patrick possibly send him to his doom by executing his plan?

Patrick apologized to Delton in his mind. The plan was essential. It had to be done for him to live. Survival can really change a person.

Martha was cursing herself for accepting the offer to be a crew member. She knew Alan could not be blamed, but for some reason, she felt it was because of him. Perhaps his meeting with the Harandel in Jakarta was the reason behind the happenings on the island.

Alan still had one last trick up his sleeve. Now that they were sure, him and Andrew were the ones, they started discussing about choosing the right time to executed he plan. Andrew had said, "We should do it just moments before it will be too late. That will force the Harandels to make a choice fast." The two men had agreed on this.

At least they had completed the first step. The cube had been placed in the entrance by sunset. Now it had to be opened before the deadline that the Harandel had warned them about.

Bardos was still chanting by the stone column when they heard a roar not too far from there. It sounded just like the troll's. The mere sound of it made the crew shiver.

It took ten minutes for Bardos to finish his spell. He turned to the others and said in a dull tone, "Its done. The entrance shall open soon." Andrew couldn't resist and asked, "Did you hear that roar Bardos? Was it a troll?" Bardos the watcher swallowed and said, "Yes. Before you killed the troll and expelled Antrosel from that body, in a final act of rage, he made the troll call out to its brethren. They are coming. My only hope is that they will not reach in time to cause any problems."

Antrosel's name sparked a thought in Alan's mind. He had said they would meet again. It would be sooner than Alan thought. What had he meant?

A few minutes passed. The crew was waiting for the entrance to open Then seven massive figures burst through the trees. They were trolls, just as they had expected. One of them was even larger than the others. Probably the alpha.

Alan, Andrew and Bardos stepped back. The others just watched with a bored expression. They were going to die anyway, why should they have cared?

The trolls didn't seem interested in to crew either. They assumed them to be dead animals. It would be wiser to kill the live ones first.

Alan looked at Andrew and Bardos. Their faces turned pale. Their brows were beaded with swear. Alan himself was no less terrified. Defeating one troll was tough enough, but seven?

Bardos snatched a staff from thin air. The plain wooden stick had nasty blade at its end, but Andrew doubted it would do much against a troll.

The trolls edged closer with surprising coordination. It didn't take too long for the three to realize that the trolls were herding them into a death zone. A death zone didn't exactly appeal to Alan. The trolls had formed a circle around them. They had absolutely no where to run. Their luck was meant to run out eventually and it had.

Alan had nothing to defend he myself with. Even a sword would have been fine. Though it wouldn't be much, at least he would have a weapon of some sort. Now he felt vulnerable and exposed.

Bardos leaned close to Alan and Andrew, then whispered into their ears, "Run when I tell you." They weren't sure how he was going to do it, but nodded.

Bardos took a few steps away from them. The tip of his staff seemed to glow, successfully distracting the trolls.

Two eager, young trolls advanced. This was the first time the crew witnessed the true extent of the watcher's powers. A bolt of white energy shot our from the glowing tip. It made a beautiful contrast with the black sky above. The troll came crashing to the ground. He fired a second shot which hit the other one square in the chest. It was thrown twenty wards away into some trees which were completely destroyed.

Alan and Andrew almost thought that Bardos would simply shoot each of them down, but the blasts had drained all his energy. He would have fallen down if it hadn't been for his staff. He leaned against it, coughing.

Alan and Andrew ran to support the boy, for once, completely forgetting the trolls.

Patrick and the others had been watching this with awe. They too had faced a troll courageously just that evening and now, they were watching their friends struggle, doing nothing. They couldn't sit and watch anymore. Their death was now inevitable. They might as well do something to be remembered for by their friends.

They stood up and ran towards the trolls. The trolls had been startled and actually stepped back. Their previously dead meal was charging at them. The predators who had never faced this situation before didn't know how to handle it.

The trolls were stupid, but not that stupid. They recovered soon and also charged at the crew. The two groups were separated by a mere fifty metres when a blinded flash turned night into day.

Everyone froze in their places. The well was the source of the light. It dimmed just a bit for them to make out the silhouette of a dragon. The trolls stumbled backwards and fell over each other. All eyes were fixed in the Purple Harandel that had emerged from the entrance.

Patrick couldn't help smiling. Soon he would be saved.

Alan took a step towards the entrance when the island shook beneath their feet. It had begun.

"Alan, Andrew…go!" said Bardos. They looked at each other. Their expressions conveyed a simple message, *Its time.*

They had barely walked a few feet when a voice called from behind them, "I don't think you're going anywhere." It was Patrick and he was holding a pistol. He had taken two gun from the pirates, knowing that he would need it. He had used only one of the guns in front of the others. This one had been safe in his pocket.

Patrick continued, "There are six bullets in this. One for each of you…I'll be the only one going through that entrance."

This was not going good. Alan had to think of something and fast. The best course of action would be to stall Patrick for a while. "Patrick, what's gotten into you and what do you mean by six of us? There are only five of us." Patrick chuckled and replied, "There are six of you Alan. Andrew, Martha, Delton, Alex, you and Bardos."

The crew couldn't believe this. Alex reacted first, "You'd murder your own brother?" Patrick's reply was the he didn't like competition. Martha had stopped crying. Now she was filled with rage. "Patrick, how could possibly even imagine killing Bardos? He almost gave his for us life fighting off those trolls just now."

Patrick Maple laughed. There was madness in his eyes. He said, "I am not going to kill Bardos just yet. I still need to know how to get through the entrance safely." Bardos spat and replied, "I'd rather die before I betrayed the Harandels. There is no use threatening to take my life. Apart from that, you can't just jump into the well and pass through. Only I know the way to pass to the other side alive." "I expected you to be smarter. You just revealed that you have information I need. So I'll not threaten to take *your* life." Patrick turned the gun towards Alan and said, "I'll threaten to take his."

Patrick walked closer to Alan and pressed the cold metal barrel against his head.

"So Bardos," he said, "tell me. How do I get through." Before he could open his mouth to say something, a flare like the one they had seen the day before they had come to the island. This held Patrick's gaze long enough. Alan punched him in the face. He dropped his gun and fell to the floor.

Bardos smiled, "Good job Alan. Now let's go, c'mon." Alan was about to say something, but was interrupted by a troll who had walked up to them. It seemed to ignore them and walked straight to where Patrick was. He picked up the screaming man and ran back into the forest. The other monsters followed this one and they were gone.

"I won't go.", said Alan. "Nor will I" stated Andrew. Bardos was baffled, "What do you mean?" "We won't go through the entrance until you guarantee the safety of the others."

Alex, Martha and Delton's respect for Alan and Andrew increased tenfold. All this time Alan had been thinking of a way to save them. "Alan…" Martha began.

Bardos interrupted and said, "Alan its not possible." Andrew replied to this, "We know those Harandels need us. For what reason, we are unaware, but if they want us to come, they need to save our friends."

Bardos sighed and closed his eyes. A few moments later, he opened them and at that very moment, the inventor, the astrophysicist and the biologist had vanished into thin air.

Alan looked at Bardos, "What happened?" Bardos assured them, "They are safe. The Harandels will ensure it."

Bardos walked to the well. "Alan, Andrew, all you have to do is jump into the well." "But you told Patrick…Oh, impressive." said Andrew.

The two of them stood on the wall of edge of the well. Alan noticed that Bardos wasn't there with them, "Aren't you coming?" Bardos smiled and said, "This is where my part ends. The Harandels are waiting for you. Hurry."

The two friends closed their eyes and jumped.

Chapter 15

A New Tale Begins

Before I explain this part, I must add that it wasn't included in the first message that I revived from Mr Sawner.

Delton, Martha and Alex woke up in an extensive field of grass. All of them remembered what had happened. Patrick going crazy, Alan and Andrew trying to convince Bardos to save their lives and the trolls carrying Mr Maple away. Then there had been a flash and they went unconscious.

When the three of them had woken up, they were here.

Martha had been the first to speak, "Where are we?" Alex shook his head. Delton looked up to the heavens for an answer. For a second, he thought he saw Alan and Andrew's faces. Then he dismissed the thought as it was impossible.

They decided to start walking in a random direction, hoping to find civilization. The sun was bright and the air was humid.

They wondered where they were. The Harandels were magical, that was for sure. What if they and been transported back in time? Delton immediately expelled this though. He was an astrophysicist and knew that traveling back in time was impossible, magic or not. What he didn't know was that the Harandels weren't magical at all. They just had abilities which humans couldn't explain. So, as it has been from the beginning of our race, they called it magic.

The three humans were getting pretty thirsty. As though to answer their silent plea, the moment they crossed a small hill, a river can into view. Without hesitating, Delton, Alex and Martha ran to the river and began drinking. The water was fresh. Fresher than any water they had ever tasted before. Just then a tiny fish came swimming along. The water was so clear that they could see every stone on the river bed though it had to be at least twenty feet deep.

The fish was a shade of indigo with a bit of purple. It was quite different from any fish they had ever seen. It was shaped like a tear drop and had no eyes. Instead of a tail fin, it had what looked like hooks and it had no other fins either. Just three holes on either side. Martha reached closer to touch it. Instantly air bubbles escaped at high speeds from the three holes, propelling it away.

As the three of them watched the fish leave, a voice behind them said, "Finished drinking?"

They instantly turned back and sprang to their feet. Alex had been so startled that he fell into the river. A boy was standing behind them. It was Bardos the watcher. He looked much better than he had at the entrance.

Now Bardos looked much different. He was wearing white robes and had a clam look on his face, unlike their last moments on the island.

They had thought that the watcher had been destroyed with the Tenebris Chorés island.

Delton stepped forward, reached out and placed a hand on his shoulder, checking if the boy was actually there.

Alex got out of the river and stood beside his friends. Bardos smiled gently. The very next moment, he was bombarded with questions. Martha asked, "Where are we?" Delton was a bit more concerned for his friends who were responsible for saving them. "Where are Alan and Andrew?" Alex managed to sum it all up with one word, "Explain."

Bardos sighed and began, "I know that all of you are pretty confused. Let's start with why you were sent here.

All of you weren't saved just because of Alan and Andrew. The Harandels decided that you had another part to play...not on earth, not at that time."

Delton was a bit confused (who wouldn't be?). He said, "So we're no longer on earth?"

Bardos still had a grin on his face which was becoming rather irritating. He continued, "Yes. You are not only on a different planet, but also in a different timeline. I'll skip the part as to how that is possible because it's too complicated for you to understand."

The last sentence seemed awkward coming from a kid, who was probably no older than thirteen to a group consisting of an astrophysicist, an inventor and a biologist, but Bardos was no ordinary human boy.

Bardos looked at the three of them. They were confused, afraid and fascinated by what was happening to them. He continued, "Alex and Martha, you must return to earth, but keep this in mind...you will not be returning to the same time that you left and things may be quite different. Delton on the other hand has some work here."

This was just great. Now Delton was going to be separated from his friends, who would be sent not only across space, but also time. He asked, "So I'm going to be alone here? By the way, where is here?"

Bardos could understand how he was feeling. He had felt the same way when the Harandels had asked him to leave his world and take on the responsibilities of the watcher. He said in a soothing tone, "Delton, we are now in a place called Sandrasia. There is an important task that you must complete. An enemy is approaching earth. A powerful enemy. Only if the people of earth and Sandrasia combine forces can he be fought off, but there is a problem."

Martha asked, "What problem?" Bardos replied, "Both the races have not reached the required evolutionary stage that will make them strong enough to fight him off. So the Harandels have decided to bring mass destruction upon both races."

Alex couldn't understand how this would help, "How is bringing mass destruction upon both races supposed to help them evolve?"

Bardos nodded and said, "When an entire race is on the verge of extinction, they are united by one sole purpose, to survive. This is key to evolution. They will adapt...mentally and physically."

Delton still didn't understand one part, "So what's our part to play in this?" Bardos replied, "Alex and Martha...you will be sent back to earth. Except the fact that you will arrive when half of the world's humans are dead. The hopes of the others will rest upon one person. If he fails, the world ends.

Your part is to assist him in the last leg of his journey, when he needs help the most. You must help him succeed. If he does, the human race will be stronger, wiser and more united than ever before. Then they will be ready to fight the ultimate enemy."

This was quite a lot to take in. They believed him though. Anyone who had experienced what they had on that island would. Bardos then turned to Delton. He said, "Delton, your job however is to help the lord of the Sandrasians, Sendion. You must help him fight of a deadly adversary...a lieutenant of the one who wishes to destroy your planets.

If you succeed, the Sandrasians too shall successfully evolve. Then the two races can be reunited."

Martha asked, "Reunited?" Bardos continued, "Both your races have a common ancestry. They were divided by the Harandels and sent to different worlds. Why? I don't know. Even your myths of dragons and elves are inspired by the Sandrasians. Think of the two races as brothers who have been, separated. Now they must reunite to fight a common enemy.

Now is the time. Are you prepared to do what I have told you?"

The three humans looked at each other. Then they said, "Yes." Bardos clapped his hands and two swirling portals of light opened before them. He continued, "The one on the right leads to earth and the one on the left leads to Golzamithos, the capital of Sandrasia."

Alex and Martha tuned to Delton. The astrophysicist extended his hand. Instead of shaking it, his friends embrace him. Alex said, "Don't die out there Delton."

Delton smiled, trying not to get teary eyed, "You too."

The two of them went over to the portal, took on last look at Delton and Bardos, then walked through. As of that moment, Delton was the only human on the planet.

Bardos stepped closer and whispered, though there was no one for miles, "Delton, you will have to help Sendion retrieve a relic. It is powerful…very powerful. You must be careful not to be consumed by its power. Be true to the quest. It is vital to defeating the enemy. Also, I grant you the power to understand their tongue and the power to be able to speak it."

Delton nodded to everything he said. Then replied, "I'm ready Bardos, but I have just one question. Will I ever see any human ever again?"

Bardos smiled, "Yes…sooner than you think." With that last bit of reassurance, Delton walked into the swirling light.

He kept walking. Random images swirled around him. Once, he could almost swear that he saw zombies with wings.

Eventually, he walked into a dark lane. Two buildings made of dark stone were on either side. Delton walked into another street. It was filled with people.

It wasn't until Delton got closer that he noticed that the people weren't exactly people.

Firstly their hair was white, but they looked pretty youthful. Though, the most striking difference was that their ears were pointed. They almost perfectly resembled the modern day description of elves, like the ones seen in movies.

Delton probably stood there for an hour or so. He eventually came to the conclusion that he couldn't stay there forever. He was wearing the same camouflage outfit that he had been wearing on the island which looks pretty odd.

Soon enough passer-by started staring at the vaguely Sandrasian creature in their midst. What was it? Delton saw a few Sandrasians approaching with menacing spears. He did the only thing that seemed logical, though it was the worst thing he could have done...he ran.

The guards had decided to interrogate this creature that had come into the city to see whether it was hostile. Delton had run away, which to the guards, proved that he had to be an enemy.

Delton ran down several streets and had completely forgot from where he had come. The guards were persistent and followed him no matter what he threw at them, literally.

The first difference that he notice with the streets of earth and the streets of Sandrasia were that they were no cars. Bardos had asked him to think of humans and Sandrasians as brothers. Sandrasia was clearly the cleaner brother with lesser pollution and garbage.

He also noticed, as he pushed through the crowd that people used large spheres that could be opened to store their things and rolled them around. The surprising fact was that there wasn't a wheel in sight.

This made Delton realize how close their two species were related and at the same time, how they were different.

Eventually Delton reached a dead end. The guards had him cornered. One of them spoke and Delton understood him, thanks to Bardos, "Surrender creature...prepare to be taken to the lord of Sandrasia."

Delton's job was to help Sendion. Why not let them take him anyway? He said, "Alright...take me to Sendion."

The guards took a step back. How did this creature know their language and the name of their lord? Then the hesitation vanished and they seized Delton by the arms. The astrophysicist struggled to break free (he had to act natural), but the guards were much stronger.

He was then walked by the guards through a maze of streets, until they reached a tall stone castle. It was not too different from the castles of earth. It was a tall central tower connected by bridges to six smaller ones around it. Delton was reminded of the Tenebris Chorés islands due to the arrangement of the caste's towers.

Delton and the guards entered through late wooden doors on the main tower. As they walked in, Delton noticed archers standing on top of each tower. At the moment all were aiming at Delton.

Dr Kraig was led into a spectacular throne room. The floor, walls and ceiling were all gold. There were three other doors other than the one he had entered through. At the centre was a circulars polished, white stone.

The room was filled with other golden chairs set against the walls. Each was occupied by a Sandrasian noble, except the one in the centre.

Delton was placed on his knees. One of the nobles stood up and said, "Who are you creature? Explain your not purpose in Sandrasia."

Delton swallowed and began, "I am Delton Kraig…a human sent here by Bardos the watcher."

The noble raised an eyebrow. Then said, "A human? Do you take us for fools? Humans are myths. They do not exist. Tell us the truth."

It didn't take him long to realize that just the way humans imagined elves to be myths, they had the same opinion about humans. He refused to give up and pleaded, "Believe me…I'm telling the truth." He then recounted his entire adventure on the island. From how Alan had planned the expedition to the island back on earth, their fight with the pirates, the Harandel that had saved them from the Crenobels. Their meeting with Bardos and the test. The three-legged creatures in the tunnels and he they and escaped, only to face a troll.

Then how Bardos had been snatched of the key by Antrosel up to the part where Patrick had turned on them and how Alan had saved him, Alex and Martha.

At last he ended with the part where Bardos had told him that his purpose there was to assist Sendion.

Though the nobles listened to this patiently, they didn't believe him. One of them said, "It is a good story Delton Kraig, but we have no time for stories." The others nodded. Eventually the one who had first spoken to him said, "It is done. You ought to be a spy. Execute him."

The guards seized Delton again and he began trashing about, yelling, "I'm telling the truth. Believe me."

Just before Delton was taken away, a voice behind him said, "Wait." The guards froze immediately, turned around and knelt. The nobles stood up. Delton turned around to see a person in purple robes with silver hair that seemed to glow and pointed ears like the others. The only difference were his eyes. They were a striking shade of blue. He said, "As unbelievable as Delton Kraig's story sounds, I feel it has a ring of truth. Or now I would like him to stay here as a guest, but he will not be allowed to leave."

It was pretty obvious that he was in charge. The guards immediately turned to Delton and bowed, "Forgive us for our conduct." Then back to the new Sandrasian and said, "We beg your pardon lord Sendion." The new individual walled over to the circular throne and sat down. He began, "Most of your story seems to fit into place. I for one always believed that our myths had to be based on reality. I feel that the things we believe are not real in your story are indeed real...we just cannot understand it."

Delton sighed. Finally some sensible company. Sendion continued, "Though I don't quite understand what relic it is you are meant to help me retrieve. All of our most powerful ones are sealed away. None except I can open it."

A few seconds later a guard burst into the room. He knelt, still panting and said, "My lord Sendion, the stone of Crendorkus is missing."

The sentence had quite the effect on Sendion. He stood up and ran out of the room. Delton followed. A new adventure was beginning.

Chapter 16

LARGER TRUTH

When Alan opened his eyes, the first thing he saw was the face of the red Harandel set against a grey background.

He got up and took in his surroundings. He was in a forest filled with black, dried up trees. The red Harandel was a few feet away from him. Andrew was awake and standing with the purple Harandel. The second he noticed Alan wake up, he rushed over. "They wouldn't tell me anything until you were awake."

The purple Harandel approached. He said, "Finally you're awake. I know you have a lot of questions, but be patient. We shall answer."

Alan didn't hesitate. He asked, "Are our friends alright?"

The red Harandel replied to this question, "They are safe. See for yourself."

The air shimmered before them like a heat haze. Then it seemed to change colour and an image appeared. They saw Alex, Delton and Martha standing in an open field of grass. Then the image started moving. It was like watching a movie on a high tech television screen from the future. They were walking down the field aimlessly.

One of the Harandels noticed Alan's troubled expression. "They will be fine." it assured him. The other added, "They have a major part to play in the near future." Though what it was would remain a mystery for quite some time.

The screen seemed to flicker and vanished. "Well, before anything else, I need to know why you needed us." The Red Harandel replied, "I promise to answer this question, but before I do there are some things we must tell you. You are the first humans to ever learn of this."

Andrew gulped. He hoped it wouldn't be something like, *We needed you for a sacrifice.* The purple Harandel began, "You humans theorised that your universe began from the big bang, right? Well you were partly correct. Though why the big bang occurred has a deeper explanation. To understand this, we have to trace back to the true beginning of time.

The first thing that ever came into existence was the Master. Until that point, there was nothing. Not even darkness existed till that point. The concept of nothingness itself didn't exist. There was no space and no time. None of the dimensions existed, not did matter or energy."

Alan could understand this to some extent, but he hoped Delton had been there. The astrophysicist would have been able to understand this better.

The red Harandel took over, "The Master is a being of such incomprehensible power that he could simply create or destroy matter and energy. He could create physical things by merely thinking of them. Though this seems to shatter your laws of physics, it is possible.

Though, at that point the Master was young and he hadn't quite learned to use the power he had. Anything he thought of simply popped into existence. You may even find this in some of your ancient myths. They believed so because it was true. Though these events were separated by literally countless years, the stories had been passed down through the ages.

The Master had created several realms. Realms consisted of many dimensions and each dimension had numerous bodies which you call multiverses. These multiverses contained universes."

This was quite a lot to take in. Andrew decided to ask, "So the Master created you too?"

It was the purple Harandel's turn now. He said, "No he did not. We were born the very instant the Master was. We are part of him. His hands in a sense.

Eventually as the Master grew mature enough to control his mind, creation slowed down and the realms became more stable. The Master eventually realized that he had created more than even he could focus at one time. Thus he gave us the responsibility of bringing order to his creation. We had all the knowledge in the world, we knew of everything that existed. If you're wondering, knowing everything includes knowing your language. It is essential for us to be able to communicate with every race.

We too were having trouble. To find a solution we started looking for forces that existed in every universe of every multiverse of every dimension of every realm. Soon we had found four such forces.

In fact, they are so universal that even you humans have discovered all of them. They are what you call electro magnetism, gravity, dark energy and dark matter.

To control each force, we created four beings. Elemprovous, Genardiso, Crendorkus and Shanarkus."

The last name in that list sent a shiver down Alan's spine.

Once again the red Harandel took over. He said, "These are the strongest and most ancient beings to ever be in existence, excluding the Master and the two of us.

These creatures had complete control over the forces assigned to them and could also control the other three to a certain degree. Their only purpose was to maintain balance in every realm.

After their creation, the Master began creating other beings. The strongest and wisest of these being were made the subordinates of the four governing forces.

From this point onwards the first age began. Most of the creatures had a physical form in the Masters world. What you call life is the merely the time when the Master thinks of you. The moment the Master stops doing so, you die. The Master usually makes sure that one's physical form in the world he created is properly disposed of in a natural way such as decomposition, but not a single creature on your planet has a physical form in his world.

Though all the creatures of the first age had physical forms in the Master's world. There, however these physical forms are inanimate. Their life in our world is merely because the Masters wills it to be that way.

If a creature had a physical form in his world, the Master would remember it longer which granted these creatures long lives and unrivalled power. They even had some control over the four governing powers.

The second age began when the Master created the Hontazels. They were strong and every one of them had a physical form in the Master's world.

The Hontazels that were created in this age were one of the strongest creatures in the world. Their large numbers and powers allowed them to reign over several realms. They destroyed any creature that oppose them. Though this seems cruel, we allowed it for the sake of balance to be maintained throughout the world. Not only physical forces, but also emotional forces had to be in balance because one force is related to another and a disturbance in one would cause a disturbance in the others.

Throughout this age Shanarkus, the lord if dark matter, had been observing. His belief was that he could govern the universe better with perfect balance."

Alan and Andrew had been listened to all of this with unwavering attention. It was the purple Harandel's turn once again. He said, "The third age was the most important period of the world's history. The Master ordered the two of us to retreat from the world. We were forbade from ever directly intervening with anything in the world. The governing forces were given the power to create matter which they previously didn't have.

Shanarkus took advantage of this. He created a new race called the Pentrons, as strong as the Hontazels, but more in number. They were completely under his command and had a sole purpose in life. To help their lord return balance to the universe.

At the end of this age Shanarkus, with his creations to support him, destroyed Elemprovous. He didn't just destroy his physical form in this world, but erased his essence by breaking his body in the Master's world.

The next age can be called the age of creation. Shanarkus had killed the ruler of electro magnetism, throwing that force into chaos. He claimed it as his own. Now he was not only the ruler of dark matter, but also electro magnetism. Now he had more control over the world.

Shanarkus used his new powers to create a substance called Allmatter. This substance could be moulded into anything he wished. He used this substance to create a mighty army and a powerful body for himself.

Now his ranks consisted of Pentrons and his creations made of Allmatter called Bonresels.

Genardiso, the lord of gravity and Crendorkus, the lord of dark energy noticed that the world was becoming unbalanced. They came to the conclusion that some evil had to be destroyed. As they couldn't suppress Shanarkus, they created an elite army to destroy the Hontazels.

Shanarkus was blinded by power, he had learnt to harness the energy released by destruction. He protected the Hontazels and destroyed the army sent against them. The creatures who Shanarkus had saved, joined him, adding to his strength.

The fifth age began when Shanarkus created six powerful beings, upon whom, he bestowed the power of controlling Allmatter. Their job was to build weapons for Shanarkus's mighty army. They also built large planets to is as strongholds for him.

The other two governing forces decided to act. They too created an army of beings called Kinroteps. They weren't as strong as Shanarkus's creations, nor were they that numerous, but it was all they had.

The end of this age was rather tragic. Shanarkus killed Genardiso and destroyed his essence, claiming the power of gravity too.

Now he had the strength of three governing forces. The only one to oppose him was Crendorkus who was much weaker and had an inferior army.

Crendorkus conferred with the Master. He told him to attack Shanarkus. The clash of the two forces would cancel each other's effects out even though darkness was stronger at the time.

The next two ages were times of perfect balance. They were spent by Crendorkus and Shanarkus fighting.

The seventh age came to an end with the battle of the twelfth realm. At the end of the battle, Crendorkus had been badly injured and on the verge of dying. His army had been reduced to a few thousand warriors.

If Crendorkus died now, the world would plunge into an eternal darkness. The Master would have no option except to destroy it.

The world had one chance at salvation. It was the Master himself. He intervened at the last moment and banished Shanarkus into a mere spirit form. Crendorkus also had to be sent away in order to prevent the balance from tipping.

Most of the creatures had been destroyed in the great battle of the seventh age along with their forms in the Master's world.

New creatures had to be created and the responsibility had been given back to us. This was the eight age. These creatures only existed in this world and not in the Master's.

A few still survived though. Throughout the entire world with all its realms, now only seven thousand-three hundred and eighty creatures are left who still have forms in the Master's world.

Some were descendants of the beings in lord Shanarkus's army and remain loyal to him up to this day. You have already met one of them. His name is Antrosel.

The next was the ninth age. The age in which humans were born. It ended the moment you jumped into the entrance. Yes, that was such an important point in history that it began a new age. Only time will tell why it is so significant.

By the end of the previous age, Shanarkus had found a way to return and is gathering his strength to create an entirely new form in the Master's world. If he succeeds, he'll be stronger than ever before. He is destroying entire planets to tip the balance in the favour of darkness. He will soon come to Earth. We need the two of you to help us stop the coming disaster.

We created this island as a test field to make the chosen ones face several obstacles. If they made it through, they would prove their worth.

Now that you know the truth about the past, we are ready for your questions. I believe that you now have a better understanding of the reason behind why you had to face those troubles."

Alan and Andrew's minds took a while to accept that the Harandels were telling the truth. This crash course on the world's history had changed the way both of them looked at everything.

They still had a few doubts. If the Harandel was giving them the opportunity to clarify them, why reject?

Alan asked, "Well, everything else figures out, but what was that green light in the cavern that saved us?"

For once the Harandels looked confused. The red Harandel asked, "What green light? Alan…I need to look into your memories."

Before Alan could object, the Harandel placed a claw on his forehead. In moments he could feel a presence his head. He didn't know how to explain it, but felt the Harandel. The presence was so powerful that he went into temporary shock and threw up. In his mind, scenes flashed of the events in the cavern.

The Harandel removed his claw. He looked at Alan with a glimmer in his eyes. Then said, "Alan, that green light you saw was in fact Crendorkus. He has returned." Andrew then added, "That's what the voice meant by 'if he can escape, so can I.' You said Shanarkus had returned, so I guess his return managed to even the balance out."

The purple Harandel nodded, "Good, you learn fast."

No it was time for Andrew's question. He asked, "Where are we anyway and how long have we been here?" The purple Harandel leaned closer and said, "This is a realm we created for ourselves, none can enter or leave without us allowing them to do so. Here you need no food or water to sustain you. To answer your second question, you just got here and have been here for an eternity. We created this realm in such a way that time is irrelevant here. The very concept is non-existent."

Alan needed to check on more thing, "Antrosel said, we would meet sooner than I thought. What did he mean?" The red Harandel said, "All in good time."

Andrew had one more thing to ask, "You said you needed us to help you save our world, but you still haven't explained how we can possibly have the power to help you."

The red Harandel seemed to grin. He said, "I thought you'd never ask."

Chapter 17

WE MEET AGAIN

Alan couldn't believe what he had agreed to do. The Harandel had said, "Alan, there is a chest called the chest of Apora Kalypso. It was created for Shanarkus's army in the sixth age. This ancient relic is the only thing that can save your kind. It lies in a different realm, but we can get you there. You must retrieve it."

The job seemed pretty straightforward. Go find a treasure chest. In fact, it was too easy to be true. Andrew asked, "What's the catch?" The purple Harandel arched his neck backwards, then said, "The catch is that the chest is protected by Shanarkus's new lieutenant, Antrosel. Yes, you will have to face him. That is what he meant. He knows that it is our only choice."

They didn't quite understand this. Why did it have to be them? Alan asked, "Why us? If you're as powerful as you say, why don't you do it yourself?"

The red Harandel replied, "Alan, the Master returned the power of creation to us, but we still, to this day, do not have the power to directly interfere with anything." Alan believed him, but Andrew had a feeling that there was something else that he had left out.

The only two humans there looked at each other. A moment later, they nodded. Andrew said, "Alright...tell us what to do."

The red Harandel said, "After we transport you to this place, you will have to look for a fortress. That shouldn't cause any difficulties as it is the only one on the planet and do not worry, it is a suitable environment for humans. Oxygen, and water are rather abundant. Then we need you to sneak in. Rest assured, we will guide you. Then you must avoid the guards and get into the vault which contains the chest. Hopefully you can get it back without having to face Antrosel. We wish you luck."

Alan stepped forward, "Just one last question, what are your names?"

The purple Harandel said first, "I am Loridos." The red Harandel took over, "I am his brother, Rodilos." Alan couldn't believe that the strongest beings in the world ad such ridiculous names. He almost laughed, but restrained himself due to the fear of being incinerated.

Later Alan and Andrew were escorted by Rodilos to what looked like a crop circle. "Are you ready?" asked Rodilos. Both the men shook their heads, but the Harandel didn't seem to notice.

Andrew expected something to happen. A flash, a defeating blast…something. Alan looked down and was shocked. His feet seemed to slowly melt away, but it didn't hurt. In reality, he was being transported to the other world, bit by bit.

The exact second this reached their eyes, their vision went dark.

When they opened their eyes, they were blinded by yellow light from the planet's sun. Alan and Andrew got to their feet, helping each other up. They took in their surroundings.

The humans were standing in a desert covered with what seemed to be grey sand. There was a bright, yellow sun in the sky. A few red hills were at the horizon. There was no sign of the fortress though.

They had been there only a while, but were already sweating and extremely thirsty. Andrew suggested that they head towards the hills to higher ground and try to locate the fortress. They agreed and forged ahead.

Alan still had his watch. They and been walking for seven hours with barely a few breaks. The sun had hardly moved across the sky. He may not have been an astrophysicist, but knew that all planets weren't they same. Their years and days may be much longer or shorter than earth's.

After what seemed to be an eternity, Alan and Andrew reached the hills which were much further away than they appeared. Actually it had been five hours. They were completely parched. Andrew yelled, "Water." Rodilos had said that water was abundant on the planet. Was it meant to be some cruel joke?

They walked into the shade of the hills. There was a cave nearby. Hoping that they might find an underground stream, Alan and Andrew ventured in. A few feet in, the walls of the cave seemed to glow. The reached the end, but there was no water. At least it was cooler. They leaned against the wall and sat down. Then a familiar voice said out of nowhere, "Alan, Andrew, there is water behind the cave walls. They are extremely thin…you can break them." This voice definitely belonged to the red Harandel, Rodilos.

The two men stood up and walked over to on of the walls. Alan picked up a sharp stone lying nearby. He slammed it against the wall with as much force as he could. There was now a small hole in the wall through which water gushed out. They drank as much as they could and sat down again.

A while later Alan and Andrew walked back to the mouth of the cave. The landscape hadn't changed much, except a white egg shaped craft was flying, just a few feet above the ground towards a tall cylindrical structure, that was the same colour as the sand. The fortress had appeared from nowhere.

Rodilos's voice sounded again, "You must enter that fortress. Once you get close enough, I will tell you how."

It took Alan and Andrew another hour to reach the fortress. They had even rolled in the sand to camouflage themselves.

Once they were there, Rodilos had told them to simply place a hand on the structure to open a passageway. Generally only Antrosel's warriors could do that, but now they could too, thanks to the Harandels.

Alan and Andrew entered the brightly lit corridor. The moment they entered, the entrance closed itself. The passage was white, extremely smooth and completely circular, like the inside of a pipe. Alan took one step and fell. He could barely get a good grip. Andrew wasn't faring much better.

Eventually they managed to figure out that it was easier to slide down the corridor than to try and walk. As they moved on, the corridor split into several others. They glanced through one and saw one of the egg shaped ships, just hovering there. They kept heading straight, the chest was probably at the centre of the fortress. Alan couldn't help wondering, as he kept sliding, as to what kind of creatures might use such a passage.

Alan an Andrew eventually slid into a circular room. Its walls were lined with what looked like bows and arrows. Except the arrows were already notched though no one was there. Andrew had to remind himself that they were on a different planet in an entirely different universe. There may be similarities between things here and back home, but they weren't the same. For all he knew, they might be naturally growing vegetation that looked like bows and arrows, used the way we use flowers.

They kept going for a few more minutes. Alan was surprised that his watch was still working, despite what it had been through.

Finally, they got their first view of the fortress's inhabitants. They were snake like creatures, with long black bodies. Instead of a head, their bodies separated into two necks. At the end of each was a speaker shaped structure. The entire creature reminded Alan of headphones.

Luckily, they hadn't been noticed. They kept sliding down the corridors till they became too tired to go any further. What they hadn't realized was that they had entered a passage that sloped downwards. The lack of friction prevented them from doing anything to save themselves.

It was only when the slope got too steep to escape that Alan and Andrew noticed it.

It wasn't too long before the tunnel turned into a freak slide.

The two of them screamed, not realising that it could attract unwanted attention. Luckily most of the creatures had been summoned by Antrosel to the courtroom.

At last, it ended. Alan and Andrew were thrown into another passageway. This one had a flat floor, which they were grateful for. This one, unlike the others was brown and seemed to be carved of stone.

At the end of the tunnel, illuminated by an eerie while light from above was the chest of Apora Kalypso.

Alan took a step forward, but Andrew pulled him back. He said, "Do you think the chest will be left here without any defences?" Alan shrugged. He hadn't considered it.

Andrew had pocketed the stone that they and picked up in the cave. He took it out now and threw in in front of them. It immediately exploded. Great. They had come all this way, only to see the chest and return, empty handed.

Alan said to himself, "Rodilos, help us." Andrew placed a hand on the wall and tried to see whether he could enter a parallel passage and re-enter at the spot where the chest was. No such luck. The Harandel's powers didn't seem to work in this chamber.

Rodilos's voice echoed through the corridor, "I should have seen this. Only Antrosel or one of his guards can walk through this chamber and return alive."

An increasingly regular feeling returned. Disappointment. Now what were they to do?

At that very moment, a single creature, like the one they had seen in the other corridor, slithered into the chamber.

Its heads turned towards them and it made a hissing sound. They didn't understand how it could see them without eyes, but there was no time to worry about that.

Alan did the only thing that seemed sensible at the time. He punched it. The other head turned towards him too. Andrew grabbed its neck and tried to strangle it.

It took them a while, but they managed to subdue it.

The creature's heads turned towards the two humans. It said, "You will die." Alan and Andrew were puzzled, how did it know English? Rodilos, as always was there to explain, "I have granted you the power to understand the language of any creature in the world. A small favour."

148

Andrew was trying to kill it by banging its head against a wall, when Alan said, "Stop. I have an idea." He continued, this time addressing the creature, "We'll let you go…if you retrieve the chest." It hissed, "Never." Alan sighed sympathetically, "Alright Andrew, kill it." "Wait," it yelled, "I'll get it for you."

They watched as the creature just slithered towards the chest, unharmed. It used its two heads to grab the chest, then slithered back.

Alan took the chest. He tried to open it but couldn't. "Now let me go." said the creature. Andrew lifted it by the neck and flung it back into the white corridor.

Andrew was sure they couldn't climb up. Maybe moving the chest would make a difference and they could open an entrance in the wall like before. He was right. A circular hole, large enough for them to climb through, opened up in the wall.

Alan held the chest tight as he and Andrew slid down the corridors. They had tried to open more entrances in the wall, but they just entered a different passage.

Eventually they reached a part in the corridor that sloped down again. They were afraid that they would end up back in the same chamber, but instead they slid down into a bowl shaped room. They reached the bottom, but couldn't climb back up. The corridor that they had entered through was too high. There was also another one, slightly lower, but still too high.

The tried to open an entrance below them, but nothing happened. Rodilos wasn't giving them any useful advise now either.

A while later, to their horror a single guard snake came in through one of the corridors. Soon several followed. There were at least two dozen of them. They didn't have fangs like the snakes of earth, but if one of them got to their necks, it could definitely strangle Alan and Andrew to death.

They punched and kicked the first few away, but they quickly recovered.

Now they hoped they couldn't understand the creatures' language. Some threats made by them are too sickening to mention.

Alan had the courage to fight, but his limbs refused to obey his command.

Just when it looked like they were going to be overpowered, a voice sounded throughout the room and time seemed to slow down. The voice was the same as the one that had emanated from the green light in the cavern when they had faced the troll possessed by Antrosel. It said, "Let me lend you my power, Alan and Andrew. I am Crendorkus and I have realized your importance in the time to come and that your souls are pure. I can help you, lend you my power, with your permission."

It was almost funny that a governing force was asking a human's permission. Alan and Andrew yelled in unison, "Just do it!"

The next set of events were spectacular. Alan and Andrew each had been encased in an aura of green light.

The creatures were pushed back by an invisible force and the two men began to levitate. They rose above the animals. Alan moved his hand in which he was holding the chest and a bolt of green energy shot our from his hand. The moment it hit one of the creatures, it was incinerated.

Andrew tried too with the same result. Within mere minutes, all the creatures were gone.

They had been floating in mid air when a creature, different from the others entered the room.

"What are you?" Alan asked, his voice amplified by Crendorkus's power. The creature chuckled, or at least that's what it sounded like. It said, "I am Antrosel."

A few previously missing blanks were filled. The troll's features had been morphed by Antrosel's spirit to mimic this creature's. He had been trying to make the troll as similar to his real body as he could.

Antrosel had a long, jackal like snout, horns and frightening fangs. It also had a tail with three fingers with deadly claws. Its four muscular limbs had razor sharp talons.

Worst of all…he could breathe fire. Antrosel bellowed, "You defeated me because of that stupid host of mine. You cannot defeat me alone."

Andrew was terrified, but didn't want to show his fear. "We aren't alone. Lord Crendorkus gives us his power." Antrosel stepped back and growled. Alan used this moment to blast a bolt of green energy at him. It didn't kill him, but it was effective in injuring him.

The two men, who had never possessed such power before were having trouble controlling it, but were trying their best.

The duel was pretty much a stalemate, until Alan discovered a handy trick. He pointed both hands at Antrosel and willed another burst of energy. Instead of a single blast, there was now a continuous stream of green energy.

Andrew copied his friend's action and too fired a beam of green light at Antrosel who tried everything in his power to protect himself. He tried creating a shield like he had in the cavern, but it shattered. He even tried breathing fire at it, but nothing happened.

At last, smoke started coming off of Antrosel and his body began to burn. He trashed around and howled, but they kept going. Alan and Andrew didn't stay to see the end. They willed to be flown into the other corridor and they were.

They had exhausted the power lent to them, so instead of flying, slid down the corridor until they reached on of the crafts.

Alan placed a hand on it and an entrance opened, I to which they climbed. There were no seats, so the just sat on the floor. Nor were there any controls, which meant they weren't getting out of there too soon.

"Fly already.", Alan yelled and the ship's walls turned transparent. They watched as the wall in front of them dissolved and the ship shot through it, escaping the fortress.

Despite all odds they had done it now, they had got the chest.

Chapter 18

DEATH BY MAPLE

Before getting to the part where Alan and Andrew ended up in the ocean, the incident with the crows has to be explained.

Alan and Andrew had been flying over the desert in the ship they and stolen from Antrosel's fortress. Alan had said, *fly*. And the ship had taken off too fast to control. In mere minutes it had reached an ocean.

Everything had been fine until they got distracted in a conversation. Alan had said, "Now that we have the chest, how do we get back?" Andrew had eyed the chest wearily and replied, "I think we should wait for the Harandels to transport us back."

As the conversation continued, a massive, black bird, which bore a striking resemblance to a crow, collided with the ship in mid-air.

The hull had been damaged and the craft went spiralling towards the ocean. Alan and Andrew, along with the chest had jumped out of the ship just before it crashed.

They had survived, but had lost the chest. Alan and Andrew gasped for breath as they broke the surface. Alan asked, still shocked, "Where's the chest?"

Luckily, a while later it floated to the top a few metres away. They swam towards it as fast as they could.

"Thank goodness" said Andrew. "What do you reckon we do now?" he asked. Alan shook his head and said, "I don't know." He then screamed, "Rodilos help us." No use.

After floating there for a while, they realized how thirsty they were. Andrew almost fell asleep and swallowed a bit of water. He was surprised to find that it was fresh. It had been stupid of them to assume that an ocean would be salty on a different planet.

An hour or so later, Alan felt something tugging at his foot. Then it got worse and he was pulled under. The same thing happened to Andrew who was holding the chest.

They were being dragged to the ocean floor. The two friends looked at each other, their eyes wide with panic. The pressure was becoming too high to bear...they blacked out.

When they woke up, they were in what looked like a cylinder. The chest was missing, probably taken by their captors. They heard voices outside. It was saying, "Found them on the surface. They fell from the sky in a ship like the ones which the Death Bringers use."

The top of the cylinder was opened and the whole thing was turned upside down, dropping them on the ground, covered in what seemed to be purple grass.

Two guards, about sixteen feet tall, vaguely humanoid hefted them to their feet. Each were carrying large, deadly spears. Their skin was blue and they had elongated skulls with extremely large eyes. Their limbs were long and too thin. The fingers and toes were webbed and they even had gills.

It gave Alan a bit of relief in knowing that they weren't too deep down as sunlight still reached them.

They were being walked through what looked like a market place. Hundreds of these things were crowding around Alan and Andrew to look at the two new creatures that had been found on the surface.

Alan looked up and saw that they were in a sort of air bubble held down by a transparent, glass like material.

The tallest structure visible was a tower which was probably at the centre if the city. Once they reached there, two large metallic doors swung open for them to enter.

They were greeted to a courtroom, a room with white walls, beautifully decorated with banners and the same bow and arrow like things they had seen in Antrosel's fortress. There were six black, stone chairs on either side and one grey chair at the far end of the room. Probably the king's throne. One of the creatures sat on each chair.

Alan and Andrew were forced onto their knees before the king. The king said, "Who are you? Why were you found flying in one of the ships that the Death Bringers use."

Alan finally mustered the courage to speak. He told him that they were retrieving an artefact for the Harandels from the fortress and had stolen a ship to help them escape.

Though he was hearing the truth, the king believed it was a story made up so that he would release them. He said, "You lie. There Harandels are mere myths. Tell us the truth or die." Andrew knew that there was no use telling this fool of a king the truth. He said, "Your majesty. We are warriors from a far away land. The chest we had belongs to our kingdom, stolen by the ones you call Death Bringers. We were sent by our king to retrieve it. We had no means to leave and so stole the ship. Please return the chest to us and let us leave."

Now *this* (completely fake) story made sense to the king and he believed it. His reply was, "You had no reason to lie using the name of the Harandels. Everyone knows it to be a myth. I agree to return it to you and allow you to leave. On one condition. If you are warriors, you must be trained to fight. We need you to ward off a spirit that has been wrecking havoc on our city's borders. Do this and you may be on your way."

They had to accept the king's terms. If only Crendorkus would help them now. "We accept your majesty." Alan said.

The king was overjoyed. He said, "Excellent. Now let us eat and have a good night's sleep. You leave tomorrow."

The banquet hall where they had been taken was huge. The table was lined with various exotic meats and drinks. Alan and Andrew decided to stick to what most resembled good that they were familiar with.

After that two guards had escorted then to two different rooms. The doors had been locked from the outside. Typical.

Before sleeping Alan looked out at the sleeping city through the window. This reminded him a lot of the time when he had looked out through a different window at Jakarta from his hotel after the meeting with his investors who were now far away in an entirely different universe.

The next morning, they had been woken up and taken back to the courtroom well before sunrise. The king was awaiting for them. They bowed and then stood straight. Alan said, "My lord, we need weapons. Ours were lost in the fortress."

The king nodded and clapped his hands. Two of the creatures came running. Each was carrying the bow and arrow shaped objects.

They looked like the weapons of earth, but the entire thing was completely rigid, even the string. It would be embarrassing to say that they didn't know how to use it, claiming to be warriors, so Alan came with with an excuse. He said, "My lord, from where we come, such weapons do not exist. How do these marvellous objects work?"

It turned out that by moving the end of the arrow across the string would control its strength and all they would have to do to fire it would be to tap the arrow's shaft.

Andrew tried changing the power and the previously rigid arrow moved along the string.

Then they were taken by two guards to the outskirts of the city to a dark forest. It reminded him of where the Harandels lived, but this one was different. The place itself was evil.

From that point they had to journey alone. With their new weapons in hand, Alan and Andrew walked into the forest.

There wasn't much wildlife except for a few rabbit-like creatures which tried to eat their legs. They handled them easily with their bows.

Finally they reached a house. It was strikingly human. There was something about it that seemed familiar.

It was exactly the same as Patrick Maple's bungalow, but it wasn't normal, like any real house, it had an eerie while glow to it and seemed to be made of smoke.

A ghostly figure walked out from behind the bungalow. Alan and Andrew's mouths fell open. It was Patrick Maple. The ghost that had been terrorising the city had been Patrick?

"Hello Alan, it's a pity I couldn't kill you when I was alive. Now I can make it much more painful." Patrick said. Rage welled up within Alan. He fired a shot from his bow which Patrick dodged and Alan said, "Patrick, you're a backstabbing, blood sucking leech, you know that right?"

Patrick actually laughed. He said, "Alan, you should mind your tongue. I am now a commander in Lord Shanarkus's army in the twentieth realm."

Andrew was startled. He asked, "How do you know about Shanarkus and the realms?"

Patrick replied, "You see, after the troll killed me, Lord Antrosel revived my spirit and told me everything about the world, the Master, lord Shanarkus and the Harandels. He asked me whether I wished to join the lord's noble cause to restore balance to the entire world. I accepted the job."

The only humans alive in the forest were shocked. Even when they were told of the truth about the world, they hadn't been so surprised. Patrick may have been arrogant and immature, but he wasn't a bad person. Darkness had invaded his mind and consumed him.

Patrick continued, "Lord Antrosel had promised to send you here. He kept his promise. Now…prepare to die Alan Sawner and Andrew Briston." He raised a pale, white hand. It immediately blazed with red light.

Andrew couldn't do anything to help. His only strategy was to bargain for time, hoping that Alan could formulate a plan by then. He said, "Antrosel is dead."

Patrick's grin vanished and he lowered his hand ever so slightly. He said, "You're lying. It is impossible."

Now it was Andrew's turn to smile. "You don't know, do you? We killed Antrosel."

Patrick was getting irritated. He said, "No human can kill Antrosel."

Alan replied this time, "We weren't alone Patrick. Lord Crendorkus helped us."

Patrick's form shimmered. He screamed back at them, "No. Crendorkus has been imprisoned. You're bluffing."

At the mention of the Crendorkus's a name, a few more ghosts emerged. They weren't coming from the forests, but were coning out of the trees themselves.

Some ghosts were humanoid, some were of creatures they recognised, most they didn't. One of them asked, "Crendorkus has returned?"

Andrew saw an opportunity here. He said, "Yes." "At last, our torment is over. The lord has returned." proclaimed one of them.

The other ghosts cheered. Patrick was furious now. He stamped the ground, sending a red shockwave outward.

The ghosts calmed down. Patrick yelled, "You believe these idiots? Crendorkus cannot return. Lord Shanarkus made sure of it. You know it to be true." The ghosts whispered to each other, confused.

Alan stepped forward and raised his hand. He screamed, "Lord Crendorkus has returned and I have proof." His hand erupted in green flames and Crendorkus's voice said, "It is true. My loyal comrades, fight for me once again. Alan Sawner and Andrew Briston are essential for our victory against Shanarkus. Protect them." Alan had been trying to communicate with Crendorkus while Andrew had been distracting Patrick. He had succeeded.

The ghosts charged at Patrick. He kept blasting random ghosts, but they were starting to win.

Alan almost thought they would manage to subdue Patrick. Almost. Patrick was stronger than he looked. An explosion of red energy vaporised every ghost that was there.

"Enough." Patrick yelled and said, "Your little magic tricks cannot protect you."

Alan and Andrew felt a familiar tingling feeling in their hands which now glowed dull green. They realized what was happening and smiled.

Patrick was puzzled. Why were the two of them smiling?

The answer came soon enough. Alan and Andrew raised their hands, blasting Patrick with green light. His image turned green and he started falling apart.

Patrick's face became normal, only for a moment, but it was no longer pale or ghostly. His face looked like it had on the day they had set out for the island, confident, strong and reassuring. He looked at them with a smile and said, "I'm sorry Alan. They can invade your mind and control you. I have seen what they plan to do. Be strong, you have a lot to face. I'm sorry."

With that disturbing statement, Patrick Maple was destroyed forever. Removed from the Master's memory.

Alan and Andrew swallowed. Patrick's warning had been dreadful.

The two of them walked slowly back to the edge of the forest.

Their bows were still with them as they entered the city. The king was waiting for them there with a dozen or so guards. The king asked, "So?" Alan replied, "The ghost...is gone." He was trying to decide whether to reveal the fact that the spirit destroying their city was a past comrade of theirs. He came to the conclusion that it would be better to keep it to themselves.

The crowd of creatures around them cheered. The king clapped once again. In response, two guards brought the chest of Apora Kalypso and handed it back to the two men.

"When are you to leave, young warriors?" To be honest, they didn't know. To clear this doubt, Rodilos's voice sounded again. "Alan, Andrew, it is time to return." Andrew threw his head back and sighed, "Finally you answer Rodilos. The creatures panicked and ran. Others stumbled and fell. The king could not believe what he was hearing, the story which Alan had said was true.

The king stared at Alan and said, "You weren't lying." It was that exact moment that Alan and Andrew disappeared from that planet and were transported to the Harandels' realm.

Chapter 19

ART OF DECEPTION

Alan and Andrew were conscious this time. The chest was in Alan's hand. Loridos looked at the chest with a pleased expression and said, "Good, you retrieved the chest." Rodilos who was standing next to him, extended a hand. Alan placed the chest in it. It opened on its own and a golden stone floated out. Its beauty was beyond compare.

They felt like admiring the stone all day long, but there were a few things that needed resolving. Andrew asked Rodilos, "Hey, why didn't you help us out after we left the fortress. We had to go through a hell of trouble because of that."

Loridos answered, "The balance was changing drastically. Up to that point the balance had been tilted in favour of good, but now there was a drastic rise in the power of darkness. Even now it is rising fast. Faster than ever before."

Alan was confused, how were these related? He asked, "That doesn't explain why you didn't help us." Loridos hesitated and his brother replied instead, "You see, we are connected to every opposite force. I am the representation of good and my brother is the representation of darkness. When the balance shifted, it caused such an increase in his strength and decrease in mine that we were incapacitated. The balance has been tilted in my favour so long that I had nearly forgotten how it was when things were balanced. My brother has been weak for a long time and the power was almost too much for him to handle."

Alan and Andrew felt guilty for accusing them of not helping. "We're sorry." Alan said.

Andrew was guilty too, but he needed to know something. "When you said that the Master forbade you from directly interfering in anything and that's why you couldn't retrieve the chest yourself...you weren't telling the whole truth, were you?"

Loridos seemed pleased, "You are smart for a human Andrew. We will tell you, but before that, we wish to grant you each, one chance to contact anyone you wish."

"Anyone?" asked Alan. Rodilos replied, "Yes. You may tell them anything you wish."

This was tough to decide. One might first wish to call his or her family, but Alan was expecting a trick of some sort. Before Andrew could say anything, Alan said, "We need time to think about it." The Harandels nodded and then melted into the shadows.

If time had been running the way it does on earth, they had been thinking about it for three days. Alan had asked Rodilos if he could look at the future from there. After all time was irrelevant there.

Rodilos had reluctantly agreed, but had said that they would not be allowed to look at anything that might change what they wrote in their messages.

Alan concentrated and looked into the future for a boy. The one who had asked him whether he would publish a book after this whole affair ended. It was true that this wasn't the end, but Alan decided that if he didn't survive what the future held for him, he might as well let the human world know what happened.

Alan willed to see the boy, four years from now. If Shanarkus was doing to destroy earth soon, he would have done it by then. Nothing happened and Alan dreaded that his home had been destroyed by then and every human, including the boy was gone.

An image flickered, but it didn't show the boy though. Instead it showed Alan, floating in space, next to Rodilos. He could hear his voice in his mind. "Alan, after this no human will remember anything of the last four years. Everyone and everything related to the incidents will be erased. New memories will replace the old ones. The human world will become as it was before the Tenebris Chorés islands. None of you will be remembered, but a new life is waiting for you."

None of them would be remembered and a new life was waiting for him. What was he talking about? Was Rodilos about to erase the memories of every human in existence? This was all new information. This meant that something was going to happened that humans could simply not be allowed to remember. This just made it more important to send this e-mail. If humans were unprepared when Shanarkus attacked, this e-mail might be the only information they would have to even stand a chance.

Then the image of William appeared in front of him. He was holding an iPad sitting on a beige sofa.

Alan's plan was to send everything that had happened till then as an e-mail to the boy's future self. If he was alive after four years, playing on an iPad, the world must be fine. Finally a great weight had been lifted off his shoulders. The world would have enough time to prepare if they got the e-mail or perhaps, the incidents had already gone by and they had survived Shanarkus's invasion. The question was, would this information be enough and how would it ever reach everyone?

Andrew had discussed with Alan and decided that it would be the best course of action to send all the events as an e-mail to William, requesting him to write it as a story. Andrew had one call too. He would contact his family and tell them to inform the world that they were safe.

So, the next they when the Harandels asked them whether they had decided, Alan said, "I want to send an e-mail to the future. To…to a friend." Rodilos considered, but he knew Alan had seen only what was safe to see. He agreed.

Andrew's request was genuine and pretty emotional. The Harandels agreed to grant them their wishes.

Andrew had written:

Dear mom,

    Its Andrew. Alan and I are safe. Do not worry about us. Tell Alan's family too. We cannot reveal anything for now. Please be safe.

                  With love,

                  Andrew.

Alan had read this and was touched. He asked himself, *Why me?*

The next five hours were spent by Alan writing to Willaim. He made sure to make it as short as he could, yet put as many details into it as possible.

He titled it as 'Alan Sawner" and began writing. He introduces himself by saying that he was a Scottish billionaire. He described himself standing at the entrance of the Soekarna-Hatta international airport at Jakarta. He explained that he was planning a joint venture to the Tenebris Chorés islands and even narrated the story of Christopher Marques.

Then he wrote about what had happened at the meeting and how Sheik Halmeer al-Jilani had warned him not to go to the island. He talked about his crew in great detail, all the time hoping that the boy wouldn't just delete the e-mail.

He got to the part when he had met Andrew on the highway. He also described the beach, the mansion, the lighthouse and everything else that had happened.

He also recounted their first encounter with Rodilos in great detail and also the tsunami and Jimmy Van Lee's death.

Alan explained each and everything that had happened in Portland, New York, Paris and Hong Kong before they left for the island. He even explained the part where William had asked him that question which gave Alan the idea of sending this e-mail in the first place.

He then got to the part where they had fought the pirates and barely escaped with their lives. Then he came to the part where they fought off the Crenobels and met Loridos.

Next he introduced Bardos the watcher and explained their first meeting. Writing about him made Alan wonder where he was. He made a mental note to ask the Harandels later.

Then he wrote in great detail about their underground tunnel adventure and the three legged creatures they had faced, the Crenobel in the cage and how they had escaped.

At last he cane the the encounter with the troll and how he and the late Mr Maple had rescued their friends.

Then he came to the part where Bardos had sent them back to get the key cube and how Crendorkus had helped them defeat the three legged creatures. He also mentioned how he had overloaded the acoustic blaster on purpose and blown the troll up.

Alan eventually got to the part where Patrick had pulled a gun out on him and had then been killed by a troll.

Alan got a little more serious while explaining what the Harandels had told him and Andrew about the Master and the creation of the world.

This was clearly the most important piece of information Alan had to give William.

Finally he reached the part where they had been sent to retrieve the Apora Kalypso chest. He recounted the events in the fortress and their reunion with Patrick's ghost and for to the point of writing this letter.

At the end Alan wrote:

> *You may think of this as an elaborate prank, but it is the truth. Believe it if you wish, but please make sure that it reaches the world. I know this fifteen page summary of our journey is too plain and simple to ever become popular enough to reach every human in the world, but I trust you to make it interesting and weave these incidents into a good story. I trust you my friend*
> *From the past,*
> *Alan Sawner.*

Here I, as the author must add that up to this point, I transcribed what I received in the first e-mail from Mr Sawner in the past. From here, I am writing from what I learnt in the second e-mail. When I got that and from whom is a story for another time.

Alan then thought, *send*. The image on the screen in front of him changed and now displayed the word 'sent' under a blue envelope.

The screen disappeared as the two Harandels appeared. Andrew stood up and stood next to Alan. He asked, "Well, we sent our messages. At least now could you tell us what that stone in the chest is for?"

Loridos answered, "Yes. I shall explain, but promise not to lose your temper. You see the human race has not evolved enough to survive against Shanarkus. The stone of Apora Kalypso has the power to evolve any species to a much higher level…the only thing is, it does that by eradicating a massive part of that species' population."

"You mean you're going to destroy the majority of humans on earth to make some of them strong enough to fight Shanarkus. How can you do that?" Alan snapped.

Rodilos replied, "I know it seems unfair, but Alan, sometimes there must be destruction before creation. Why we needed you… the sole purpose was that the Apora Kalypso will work only function on a particular species if the most evolved individuals of that species smash the stone and release its power."

Andrew began towards Rodilos with his fists raised, "You selfish little…" Before he could complete, Alan restrained him.

Loridos leaned back and said, "Alan death is inevitable. You must choose whether you crush the stone and save some humans or don't crush the stone and let all the humans die."

This was the same question which Bardos had asked him while testing the crew to choose the worthiest. Alan had answered that he would kill most of them of save some which was at least better than letting them all die. Now when it was actually happening, Alan was on the verge of crying. What was he supposed to do.

Andrew had acted just as brave as Alan during the test, but now he felt like his entire body had turned to lead.

Loridos raised one of his arms and a large stone cube rose from beneath the ground. It had a small, square shaft cut into one side. Rodilos threw the stone of Apora Kalypso into the shaft and summoned another column of stone that fit perfectly into the shaft like lock and key. Just a bit of it hadn't went in entirely.

Rodilos said, "Alan, all you have to do is push the column into that shaft. The stone will be crushed and the Apora Kalypso will be released."

Alan and Andrew refused. That was when Loridos said, "Alright Alan, if you can move my talon," He planted his finger firmly into the ground and continued, "you can go. I will personally fight Shanarkus and save your planet, even if it means disobeying the Master."

There were a number of different reactions. "Brother you wouldn't." Alan said, "How could we possibly match your physical strength?" "Please stop forcing us."

Loridos said, "Alan, there is another way we can do this. All I would have to do is kill you and transport the next most evolved humans here to do the job. No one can stop me from doing that." His eyes glowed purple.

Alan and Andrew reluctantly agreed. Rodilos wasn't saying much, except an occasional, "Brother, don't." They two men planted their feet into the ground and tried with all their strength. It was hopeless, how could they possibly match his strength?

Alan and Andrew then decided to try one last time. They stood about ten feet away, looked at each other and charged with their eyes closed.

The trick that Loridos had played on them was so simple, yet so effective that it was truly unbelievable.

His entire form just melted into the shadows and their momentum carried Alan and Andrew further than they had intended to go. They banged into the stone column, pushing it into place, crushing the stone and releasing the Apora Kalypso.

When they opened their eyes, the enormity of what they had done by mistake struck them like a speeding truck.

Alan and Andrew crashed to the floor. "What have we done?" said Alan.

Loridos shrugged and said, "It was necessary Alan. You will realize it when the time comes. Anyway, our work isn't done yet. We must look to the future and train the two of you to handle the power that Crendorkus has given you." These words made no sense to the two humans.

Rodilos leaned down and for the first time, looked Alan and Andrew right in the eyes. He said, "Do not despair young humans...there will be a new beginning."

Acknowledgements

My name is Sanjith Harsha Kumar, but those reading this book would know me better as William Silver. I have quite a few people to thank for the success of this book, so here we go.

Firstly, my parents for accepting to publish my book and supporting me the whole way. Of course, I also must thank my friends and the rest of my family for encouraging me.

Secondly everyone at Partridge publishing who worked hard to help me every step of the way. I'm relatively new to the publishing business and couldn't have gotten far if it wasn't for Partridge.

Last, but certainly not the least, the Frank Anthony Public School where I study and all my teachers. Especially my English teacher for choosing me to represent my school in an inter-school creative writing competition. I won it and that gave me the last bit of confidence I needed to put my story, which I had in mind for several months, into words.

Finally, I thank you, the one reading this book. Without a reader, a story isn't worth much, no matter it's potential. If you honestly enjoyed this book, please spread the word.

In conclusion, I would like to end with a request and a promise.

The request is that if you like writing and are skilled at it, no matter you're age (I'm just thirteen), write what you want and get it published. The results may be much better than you could possibly anticipate.

Now for the promise. This isn't the end. Alan's adventures will continue. William Silver isn't done yet.

Printed in the United States
By Bookmasters